Penric's
FOX

Penric's FOX

———— ❦ ————

A FANTASY NOVELLA
IN THE WORLD
OF THE FIVE GODS

———— ❦ ————

Lois McMaster Bujold

SUBTERRANEAN PRESS 2018

First Hardcover Edition

ISBN
978-1-59606-863-6

Subterranean Press
PO Box 190106
Burton, MI 48519

subterraneanpress.com

"**N**O, YOU CAN'T make a Great Earthworm!" said Inglis, sounding indignant. Although not indignant enough to rise from his comfortable recline on the mossy bank, fishing pole propped on his bare toes.

"I just did. See?" Penric held out the rosy writhing creature, flecked with moist soil, on his palm. "Isn't he cute?"

"No," said Inglis, grumpily.

The shaman's grimace failed to honor, Penric thought, the loveliest morning to escape all duties and go fishing that Pen could imagine. The quiet pool in the hills above Easthome was everything Inglis had promised his visitor: cool, tree-shaded, gilded with sun ripples. Possibly a little short of fish, but as the hazy day warmed, very inviting for a man to strip and swim. Penric had plans.

"Anyway," said Inglis, craning his neck to peer at the worm in Penric's hand, "how do you know it's a he? It might be a she."

Penric wrinkled his nose in doubt. "I've heard earthworms are both in one body."

"Oh, just like you, then," murmured Inglis, smirking.

Good to see the glum boy's not above getting his own back, commented Desdemona, amused. The Temple demon who lived inside of Penric and gave him the powers of a sorcerer was decidedly female, after all, which as he came to know Pen better had been a cause of increasing bemusement to Inglis. *Inglis kin Wolfcliff, Fellow of the Royal Society of Shamans (on probation)* as he signed his correspondence, though he hoped to be rid of the unfortunate postscript soon.

Penric tried to return a suitable sneer, but the country light was too fine to allow him to sustain the effort; it came out a grin.

Inglis shook his head. "I can't believe you mastered the technique just from watching that one sacrifice in the menagerie yard yesterday."

"That, atop reading the book you sent, your letters, talking to your Royal Fellowship and you over the past two weeks, examining, well, a few other works, half of which turn out to be rubbish. Always a problem with written sources, which frequently tell you far more about the person who wrote them than the subject addressed."

"You are a more bookish scholar than me," Inglis granted. "It seems unfair that...never mind. All right, I can see it is indeed on its way to being a Great Earthworm"—a finger reached out to dubiously prod the creature—"two souls, if you can call them that in a worm, piled into one body, but it won't arrive, and anyway, where is the point? No one would wish to be invested with a worm-spirit, and the powers it might grant wouldn't persuade a flea to jump onto a dog."

"Practice for the student shaman," Penric returned promptly. "Or student sorcerer, anyway. Earthworms are theologically neutral creatures, as far as I know. Tomorrow, I might try mice, if their tiny souls prove not too heavy for me to shift. They're vermin of the Bastard—as a learned divine of the white god I should be able to make free with them."

"Brother forfend," sighed Inglis. "Anyway, such tricks have been tried before, by people with more time than sense. After a few iterations, such lowly creatures cannot accept the overload of spirit, and die of the attempt to do so."

"Really?" said Penric, fascinated. "I must test that."

"Of course you must," muttered Inglis, with a defeated air. But he set his pole aside and sat up to watch all the same.

Pen pulled half-a-dozen more earthworms out of their bait pail and strove to get them lined up in a row on a flat stone. They resisted this fate, squirming about in a disordered manner that Pen's god the Bastard might approve, but a brief tap of uphill magic stilled them into a more military rank, temporarily. He set his first attempt at the end of the row, and rather regretfully sacrificed it into the next, persuading his conscience that it couldn't be a worse death for a worm than being impaled on a hook and tossed into deep water to drown. Four more worms down the row, Inglis was proved right, as the recipient of all this effort more-or-less ruptured when Penric tried to tip the accumulating life-magic into it. "Oh," he said, sadly. "There's a shame."

Inglis rolled his eyes.

Penric abandoned his first semi-successful effort at mastering whatever of shamanic magics he could—given that his possession of a demon of disorder would block a Great Beast of any species from ever being sacrificed into him to give him the powers of a shaman proper. Raising his rod, he squinted at his dangling hook, which seemed to have lost its bait. He sniffed and tipped the pole up to swing the line back to him, rebaiting it with one of his late sacrifices, taking consolation that the humble deaths occasioned by his imitation-shamanic efforts would not be totally wasted. He plopped his line back into the pool beside Inglis's.

After a few minutes, he observed, "We are both Temple mages, though of different sorts. Why are we fishing in such an inefficient manner?"

"Because if we applied our magics, we'd be done before the wine gets cold," said Inglis, amiably gesturing at the glazed jugs set to bathe in the rippling shallows.

"Point," agreed Penric.

"Refill?"

Securing his pole with a couple of stones, Pen rose to retrieve a jug. He topped up both their beakers, tapping out the last drops into his host's cup, then rummaged in the basket for a bite more of that good bread to go with it. The purpose of going fishing was not, after all, only to catch fish.

After a little still-fishless silence, beguiled by the local wine that lay like liquid gold upon their tongues, Inglis mused, "I wonder if such limits apply to demons as well? Is there an upper range of accumulating lives, or souls, that a demon can take up and transfer along with it, as it is handed off from rider to rider at the ends of their lives?"

Penric blinked. "Good question. Although it is not souls, exactly, that a demon accumulates from its successive sorcerers. Or not usually, unless the transfer goes badly and rips the dying person's soul apart. Because any number of sorcerers and sorceresses are signed at their funeral rites as being taken up by our god just like anyone else. Not sundered from Him, certainly, or the creation of Temple sorcerers would be the blackest sacrilege. I prefer to think of my demon's personalities as images of my predecessors, like printed pages pulled off an inked plate and bound into a codex, except...more so. Else my head would be very haunted."

Inglis turned toward Penric, cleared his throat, and came out with, "Desdemona, do you know?"

It was rare that Inglis attempted to talk to Des directly, like another person, and Pen smiled in approval. He'd get the shaman trained yet. He yielded control of his voice to his permanent passenger, quite as interested in the answer as Inglis.

Des was quiet for so long Pen began to think she would not reply, but at last she spoke, necessarily through Penric's mouth. "You children ask the most bizarre questions. There is a steady attrition of demons in the world, either hurried out of it by certain Temple rites while a young elemental, barely formed, or removed with more difficulty by a saint should they ascend and go rogue when they grow older and stronger. In over two hundred years, I have shared twelve lives with my riders, ten of them human—"

"Twelve half-lives, really," Penric glossed for Inglis's benefit, "since you have never jumped to an infant or child."

"Jumping to an infant would be a recipe for disaster," opined Des. "Instant ascendance, since the mewling creature would not have the developed will and knowledge to control its demon. Very bad choice. Anyway, as I was about to say before you interrupted me—"

"Sorry."

She nodded with Pen's head. "I have not met a demon older than myself for a long time."

"That would make sense," said Inglis, trying to follow this. "The older anyone gets, the more people are junior, and the fewer senior." He frowned. "It must be strange to be oldest, to outlive all one's generation. Yet some person in the world must be that one, at every moment. Do you think you could be eldest among demons, Desdemona?"

"Certainly not!" she said tartly. But Pen sensed an unspoken hesitance in her.

"So what happens to the eldest demons?" pursued Inglis, logically. "Do you suppose they reach a point where no head can hold them, and they jump one time too many, and, ah..." His finger pointed to the exploded earthworm.

"Eeeww," said Penric and Desdemona together. "Really, wolf-boy!" said Des, and Pen went on, "I should think if that were the case, the Temple would know of the hazard, and it would have been part of my training in seminary."

"I suppose so," said Inglis, giving up his horrifying hypothesis with apparent reluctance. He took another swallow of wine, then jiggled his pole.

I would place a bet, murmured Des, *which of you gives up first and starts using your magics to cheat the fish, but I've no one to bet with.*

What, you have your whole sisterhood in there, Pen returned. *You could start a pool.*

*There's a thought…*but she broke off and glanced at Inglis, who had sat up and turned his head, listening intently. Penric discerned nothing but the pleasant summer sounds of the woodland and stream, but he knew Inglis's Great Wolf gave him preternatural hearing. Soon enough, the thump of trotting hooves sounded from the rutted road where they'd left their hired cart. The hoofbeats stopped, a low voice soothed the animal, and then quick footsteps approached on the path to the pool.

"Ah. There you are." Locator Oswyl's voice sounded strained as Pen twisted around to wave. "Five gods be thanked."

"Oswyl!" Inglis greeted his unlikely friend as well. "You made it after all!"

The senior locator from the Father's Order had been invited to make the third of their fishing party this morning, but he'd sent a note at the last minute saying that he'd been called out on an urgent new inquiry, and not to expect him. He still wore the gray vest with the brass buttons that caused Easthome inquirers to be dubbed *Grayjays*, but it hung open over his sweat-damp shirt. Done for the day, or just surrendering to the heat?

"Did you wrap things up so soon?" asked Penric cheerily.

Oswyl made his way to the streambank, planted his fists on his hips, and sighed. "No. Unfortunately. Quite the opposite. I am in urgent need of a Temple sensitive, a sorcerer even more, and you two are the closest. I am sorry, but I must conscript you."

"No time to even take a cup?" Pen asked, looking with regret at the second jug cooling in the stream.

"No time for anything. Not six miles from here, I have a dead sorceress on my hands. Murdered, I think. Sometime late yesterday or last night."

Pen, startled, stood up. "That," he said slowly, "would be a very hard trick to bring off. Speaking from personal experience."

"Someone did. One arrow through a person could be a hunting accident. Not two. And I don't think she could have shot the shafts into her own back, not even with sorcery."

"Ah." Penric gulped, and called to Inglis, "I'll harness the carthorse, then, while you gather up things?"

Inglis nodded, already bringing in their poles. It was the best division of labor, since despite his excellent horsemanship Inglis's wolf-within tended to make even such slugs as the livery nag nervous.

Oswyl, jittering with impatience, followed Pen out to the narrow hill road where his own sweating mount was tied to a sapling. "I will give it this. The scene is fresh. Usually, help from the Father's Order is called in days late, after the local authorities have strangled all sense in a mess of their own making. This improves the chances of you or Inglis sensing something useful, yes?"

Pen had no idea. But as he strode over to untether their hired horse and back it into the shafts, his most alarmed question was not who had killed a sorceress, or how, or even why, but rather, *Where is her demon?*

OSWYL'S SIX miles cross-country turned out to be closer to nine back, by the time they'd retraced their cart track, cut across some farm ways, and found a better road leading up toward a hill village. They turned aside before they reached it, then were forced to leave their cart when the side track into the steep woods dwindled to a path. But only a few hundred panting paces along it the trees opened up into a clearing.

It was a pleasant enough glade, the by-now early afternoon light filtering down green-gold through the leaves. Less pleasant was the slumped, muddled figure toward the far edge, and the buzzing of the flies being waved off by the anxious junior locator left on guard. She was using a long, leaf-tipped branch to do so, leaning back as far as possible. Not due to any rotting reek yet, Pen thought as they drew closer; she was more likely spooked by the triple braid in white, cream and silver pinned to the figure's shoulder marking a sorceress.

"My assistant, Junior Locator Thala." Oswyl gestured, by way of introduction, and asked her, "Anything occur since I left you?"

"No, sir," said the guard, rising with obvious relief. She was much younger than Oswyl's thirty or so years, looking even more fresh-faced than Pen.

"Where's that dedicat?"

"He went home to fetch us both something to eat. He should be back soon."

"The body was found early this morning by a lay dedicat from the temple at the village of Weir," Oswyl explained over his shoulder to Pen and Inglis, "sent out into the woods to check snares. This tract belongs to Baron kin Pikepool, they tell me, but he grants the temple-folk gathering rights to deadfall and small game in it, by way of quarter-day dues."

Penric squatted in the place the young locator gladly yielded to him, and peered.

The woman lay on one side, as if sleeping. Her coils of brown hair were fallen loose, a beaded cloth cap snagged awry among them. Neither fat nor thin, tall nor short, comely nor ugly; she might be in her early forties. Whatever mind had enlivened her face—and the divine's braids testified it must have been a keen one—was gone now, leaving her features bland, waxy and still. Enigmatic.

She was not dressed in formal robes, but rather, everyday garb, an ordinary dress with a thin blue coat thrown atop, to which her braids were pinned. It had not protected her clothing from the flood of blood that had soaked it and dried brown. Almost as much had gushed around the arrowhead that protruded from her stomach as from the two fletched shafts standing in her back. By the blood trail on the ground, she had fallen only a few feet from where she had been shot. *A quick death. That, at least*, thought Pen, trying to control his dismay. No sign that she had been otherwise molested.

Inglis looked over Pen's shoulder, his nostrils flaring, possibly at the disturbing smell of the blood. Thick enough for Pen to discern, it was likely overwhelming to Inglis's wolf-within, or at least his face had gone a little rigid.

Oswyl cleared his throat, pointedly, and Pen, rising to look around, thought, *Des, Sight, please.*

Pen half-hoped to find the woman's ghost still lingering, fresh enough to still appear much as she had in life; a sudden and violent death was very apt to produce that effect. Most ghosts could not speak, but a sufficiently distressed one, still reverberating from its abrupt separation from its sustaining body, might sometimes grant to a sighted sensitive a sort of dumb-show. It was a very dangerous liminal state, as the soul could slip into a permanent sundering from its waiting god that was unwilled by either party. So Pen also half-hoped not, for the woman's sake. More usually, soul and god found each other at once, and the only function of a funeral rite was to confirm the destination.

The living souls in the clearing were all vivid enough, congruent with their bodies. Inglis's bore the added spiritual density of his Great Wolf, unsettling if one didn't know what it was. Or maybe even if one did. Penric slowly turned, scanning with sight and second sight together, but found no convenient miming ghosts. Lost souls usually attached themselves to a place, rarely to their own bodies; the strange shamanic practice of carrying away the ghost of a slain spirit-warrior bound to a sacred object did not apply here. Nor was there any sign of the stray demon, not that Pen expected it. Demons could not, after all, jump to trees, which were the only other living things about. The demon must have been carried off by its new host. And *there* was a pressing question or five.

Pen signed himself in the tally of the gods, let his Sight fade, and turned to Oswyl. "No ghost. No demon. No help. Sorry."

Oswyl huffed the sigh of a man perpetually unsurprised that his luck was not in. "Worth checking."

"Very much so."

"Can you tell anything else?"

Inglis's hand tracked the line from the arrow shafts into the woods, seeking the archer's vantage, but then he shook his head. "No saying how much she turned as she fell."

Pen crossed his arms and stared down at the woman. "A few things. She's young, to start with."

Oswyl cocked his head. "Surely not. Middle years."

"I mean young for a Temple sorceress. The Bastard's Order does not usually invest a trained woman aspirant with a demon until she is done childbearing, or at least is sure she wishes no child. The chaos that demons usually shed"—Pen paused to choose a delicate term—"thwarts conception."

Oswyl's brows twitched up. "For some, that would be a benefit."

"True. But a female sorcerer must be extraordinarily clever, attentive, and experienced to successfully manage a demon and a pregnancy both at once. Some few have done it, but it's not a recommended path. So the greater likelihood is this woman has not borne her demon long."

"I don't see any spent arrows," noted Inglis, craning his neck. "Two shots, two hits. Suggests an expert bowman."

"Or bow-woman," murmured the listening assistant, almost inaudibly.

"Or he collected them after," said Oswyl.

"Mm."

Pen eyed the arrows' penetration. "He was either close, or had a bow with a really strong draw. If the latter, probably a man. I think not the former." He cast the junior locator an apologetic nod.

"Why not?" asked Oswyl—intent, not skeptical.

"One reason to murder a sorcerer that leaps to my mind"—Penric cleared his throat—"is to steal their demon."

Inglis's head turned at this. "People really try that?"

"Yes," sighed Pen.

"It wouldn't work with a Great Beast!"

"Lucky for shamans. But if the killer was after the demon, he'd want to be as close to the sorcerer as possible. A knife, not a bow, would be the weapon of choice. About the only way one could get more distance is by that Roknari trick of a throwing the sorcerer into the sea with a leaking cushion and sailing away as fast as possible. A bow suggests a murderer who very much did not want to be lumbered with his victim's demon."

Oswyl frowned. "What's the range that a demon can jump?"

"It," Pen began, but then realized he didn't have to offer a guess. "Desdemona, can you speak to that?"

"It varies with the strength of the demon," said Des, "but a long bowshot would certainly stretch it to its limits."

Oswyl's eyes narrowed as he stared back and forth from the body to the encircling woods. "Or there were two. The bowman at a distance, the other close up." He did not look as if the thought pleased him.

It wasn't an impossible scenario, and it did account for the demon, Pen had to grant.

"It had to have happened before dark last night," suggested Inglis, "to make that shot—twice—at that range."

"Unless she bore a lantern," said Oswyl. Everyone looked around. No lantern lay broken or rolled away, but it might have been carried off like spent arrows.

"A sorcerer can see in the dark," Pen pointed out. "She might not have needed one."

"A bowman can't," said Inglis, clearly still taken with his own theory.

"Unless he's another sorcerer," put in Pen. "Although in that case, he wouldn't need to keep his distance."

Oswyl groaned. "Anything else you can tell me?"

"A sorcerer is very hard to kill," Penric began, rather in the teeth of the evidence before them.

"Sorcerers with experienced demons are very hard to kill," Desdemona corrected this, "if their demons wish to protect them. A young demon will be less adept. But if any demon wishes to throw off an unwanted rider, it's not any great challenge."

Three people stared at him oddly. Penric went on in a louder voice, "What I was *about* to say is, that suggests this sorceress was taken by surprise, by ambush, and so was her demon."

Oswyl rubbed his toe into the dirt, his expression growing distant with this visualization. "Or the murderer was someone she trusted. Or murderers, gah."

Penric grimaced, a little sickened at the picture of the woman, or anyone, really, lured out and so betrayed. "I suppose so."

Oswyl's head tilted as he studied the body. "I suppose she really *was* a sorceress? Speaking of complications. Because anyone could throw on a coat with a braid pinned to it. Or pin one on someone."

She'd certainly been wearing the coat when she'd died, by the blood soaking it. Penric knelt and fingered the braid, which was stiff and clean, comparable to his own after less than its first year's use. *Des...?*

Oh, yes. There is...an emptiness, here in this husk. Hard to describe, but distinctive enough. As if the place where the soul had resided is stretched larger than usual.

Huh. Pen said aloud, "Yes, she was. Which means that the chapterhouse of the Bastard's Order in Easthome should house a bailiff of sorcerers who is her master, and who can identify her. I expect a great many of our questions may be answered there."

He tested her hand for rigor, something that Oswyl had doubtless already done, and had more practice at than Pen, too. The stiffness might be starting to pass off, but then, the day was warm. *Amberein? Helvia?* he called on the two sorcer-ess-physicians numbered among Des's prior riders. *Can you add anything?*

Helvia answered, *Not really. Too many vari-ables. Late yesterday or last night may be as close as you can come.*

Pen blew out his breath and stood up. "I do wonder why she was just left like this. Surely the murderer could have delayed discovery, perhaps indefinitely, by digging some shallow grave. He'd had time. Or hadn't he, and in that case, why not?"

"Add the question to the list," said Oswyl. "I promise it won't be the last. Meanwhile, spread out and see if there is any more this clearing has to say. Mute things may sometimes give more telling testimony than witnesses. And then we'll take this poor woman home."

Pen walked about, looking, and Des looked through his eyes. He mostly found a great deal of nothing. No lantern, no footprints, no dropped objects. No demon. Oswyl's dual-murderers idea seemed ever more plausible. "Or," he commented to Oswyl aloud, "it could have been one murderer, of either sex, and one hired mercenary with a bow. Such ruined men will kill for surprisingly little money."

Oswyl grunted. "I hate those instances. With no connection to the dead person, men like that are hard to trace."

Circling the body once more, Penric mulled, "I have to...not take it back, exactly, but—a sufficiently expert bowman might put two shafts in the air at once, possibly before he realized that shape in the gloaming was a woman and not a deer. And then, horrified at his deed, run off. Accounts for everything." *Except the demon.*

"How likely is this?"

City-bred Oswyl was no archer, Pen recalled, despite his other skills. "I could have, when I was in practice. Well, I hope not the part about mistaking a woman for a deer."

"That's a very tempting simplification." Oswyl didn't look like a man tempted. He looked like a man who had just bitten into something with a bad taste. Again. "I won't dismiss it from the list just yet. But it needs verification. *Everything* needs verification."

The lay dedicat from the village arrived, carrying a basket and leading an older woman. She turned out to be the Weir temple's divine, the one who had sent so directly to the Father's Order when her lad had come gasping back to her at dawn with news of his find. The assistant locator accepted the basket gratefully, diving into it for the food, some of which she pressed on Oswyl. Oswyl munched standing— from his prior knowledge of the man, Pen was fairly sure he hadn't yet stopped to eat today.

The local divine solemnly examined the dead woman, and agreed with her dedicat that the corpse was no one they'd ever seen before, no member of her village flock or from the farms round about. *A stranger up from Easthome,* her tone implying the Hallow King's seat was a dangerous sort of flesh-pot where one might find murderers or worse on any corner. It made Des snicker. *You could fit five of Easthome in the capital of Darthaca, and ten in old Imperial Thasalon. She has no idea what a fleshpot is. Pretty city, though, I'll grant it that.*

Inglis, who had gone off to take a wider circuit through the woods, still looking for the bowman's stand, came back then with a third arrow in his hand. Thala watched him curiously.

"Aye, same fletching," Inglis muttered, comparing it to the shafts in the corpse's back. "It was just standing in the soil"—he pointed into the trees where the slope fell toward a distant secluded stream—"but there was a bit of this stuck to it."

He offered up a tuft of coarse ruddy hair. Pen took it and sniffed. "Fox."

"So I make it," agreed Inglis.

Everyone stared at the scrap, doubtless all trying to fit it into the multiplicity of scenes they'd imagined to account for the abandoned body. Oswyl finally shook his head and took charge of the shaft, and Inglis pocketed the fur. And then they all joined in the task of carrying the woman's body to their cart. The local divine signed a melancholy blessing upon it as they arranged it in the limited space as decently as possible.

Pen turned the cart around to head back downhill, swinging aboard as Inglis took up the reins and urged their tired horse into motion once more. The two locators mounted and fell in behind, making a rudimentary sort of cortege.

Pen hoped they'd learn the woman's name soon. He was uncomfortable thinking of her as just *the corpse*, not that every person wouldn't share that demotion in time. They turned onto a wider road, and the carthorse, perhaps recognizing the way home, began pulling less dispiritedly. Oswyl rode up beside Pen.

"We really have to find that demon," Pen told him.

Oswyl shrugged. "Bastard's Order business; I yield it to you. The problem of justice for this dead woman presses more on me than concern for a creature who by its nature cannot die."

"Well, then, you might also reflect that the demon was the closest possible witness to the murder."

Oswyl's brows flew up. "Can a demon be a reliable witness? How in the world could it be called to take oath and testify?"

"It would depend on the demon. Desdemona could."

Oswyl took this in, nonplussed, then shook his head, muttering, "Magic dogs. Demons. I swear to the Father, my inquiries never used to be this strange." Distancing himself temporarily from the tangle, he pushed his horse ahead.

EASTHOME, LYING along the river Stork, was already outgrowing the city walls rebuilt just a generation ago. The crude hearse and its escort circled through the outlying houses to the south gate, which put them closest to the heights dubbed Templetown, overlooking the red-roofed spread of Kingstown below. Penric and Inglis dismounted from the cart to give the balky horse less load to pull uphill, and also to keep it moving along through the more crowded streets. Passersby stared at the body inadequately wrapped in the picnic cloth, eyed the two Grayjays riding behind, swallowed any urge to call questions, and signed themselves.

The chapterhouse of the Bastard's Order lay two streets behind the great stone bulk of the city's, and the Weald's, main temple. The old wooden merchant's mansion that had formerly housed the servants of the white god had burned down twenty years ago, and been replaced with a fine new edifice, built more to the purpose, in the cut yellow stone of this country. As the chief chapterhouse of the realm, and in close competition with its sibling Orders for the other four gods, its architecture was high, balanced, and austere, not nearly as makeshift as the more provincial chapterhouses Pen was used to. It made him feel rather provincial himself.

Thala went to pound on the door and summon the porter. Despite the heat of the late afternoon—early evening by now in the long summer light—Oswyl paused to reorder his shirt and button up his vest before turning to help the other two shift the body out of the cart. The porter emerged, straight-backed in his tabard with its emblem of two white hands, fingers curled and thumbs out, pointing both up and down. He opened his mouth to demand the visitors' business, but it stayed open in dismay as he took in their burden. "Oh, no," he breathed. The recognition was instant; clearly, they'd chosen the right destination for the dead woman.

"First," said Oswyl to him, "let us get her off the open street."

"Aye, sir." The porter gave way at once, admitting them to a spacious stone-paved hallway where they lowered their sad freight to the floor.

"Her braids declared her one of yours, and gave her rank and calling," said Oswyl, "but told us nothing else. Can you give us her name?"

"Aye, sir. That's Learned Magal. She's been missing all day, and her bed was not slept in, but we thought she'd just gone to visit one of her children."

"Do you know when she last left the house? Or when you last saw her do so?"

"She was in and out several times yesterday. I don't really remember if, if they don't match up. The night porter might have more to add. He comes on in an hour."

Oswyl nodded. "I understand she has an overseer of sorcerers here. He or she should probably be the first informed."

"That would be Learned Hamo. I'll fetch him down at once, Locator." He stared, still shocked, at the form at their feet. "Where did you find her?"

"In a wooded tract in the hills, about ten miles out of Easthome," said Oswyl, watching the porter's face.

It crimped in confusion. "Whatever was she doing there?"

"Not a place she usually frequents, then?"

"Not as far as I know, sir. Here, I'll get the Learned." The shaken man hurried away up the stairway.

He came scuffing back down very soon followed by an older man, gray-haired, in the workaday robes of a divine. It didn't take the silver cord in the braids pinned to his left shoulder to tell Pen what he was, and Desdemona controlled a slight stiffness.

Will you be all right with another demon this close? Pen asked her in worry.

Oh, aye. At this rank, we are both tame Temple demons. Think of it like two people's spouses who can't abide each other, but feign civility for their mates' sakes.

Hamo's mouth, too, fell open in a huff of dismay at what lay in his hall. "No mistake, then."

"The locators brought her in, sir, and, um... these gentlemen," the porter supplied. That last was probably meant as a politeness, given Pen's and Inglis's grubby day-in-the-country garb, but he left his superiors to sort themselves out, stepping back. Though not very far.

Hamo knelt to touch the woman's face, then signed himself, lips moving in some short prayer.

His jaw clenched as he took in the blood and the stubs of the arrows. He rose and turned to Oswyl, face more deeply lined than a moment ago. "What happened?"

"Her body was found by a lay dedicat of the village temple..." Oswyl went on to summarize the early morning's events, how he came to be called out on the inquiry, and what he'd first found in the clearing. "I could see at once I wanted a Temple sensitive, and I knew Shaman Inglis and Learned Penric to be fishing not far from there, so I conscripted them to my aid."

A look of relief came over Hamo's face, as the uncanniness he could very well sense about the two strangers was slotted into a settled place. He might not know Inglis, but he obviously was well-up on his colleagues and rivals in magics across town at the Royal Fellowship, for he merely nodded and said, "Shaman Inglis. You bear a Great Wolf, I think?"

"Yes, Learned," said Inglis, returning the nod in like kind.

"Shaman Inglis has some prior experience in my inquiries," added Oswyl on his behalf. Of course, he didn't say on which *side*. Inglis controlled his wince.

"And, Learned Penric...?" Hamo's face held the usual doubt, given the way the claimed rank clashed with Penric's apparent youth.

"Learned Penric of Martensbridge"—Penric favored him with a short bow—"court sorcerer to Princess-Archdivine Llewen of Martensbridge. I followed in Her Grace's train on her visit for her great-nephew's name-day ceremonies, and some other Temple business here in Easthome she means to accomplish at the same time." Given that Llewen was aunt to the Hallow King, and the mewling infant in question his newborn heir, Pen, too, left Hamo to sort it out for himself.

"Ah!" Hamo sounded enlightened rather than taken aback. "I believe I have heard something of your story." His eyes narrowed. "You inherited Learned Ruchia's demon, yes? I thought I recognized that extraordinary density."

"You knew Ruchia?" asked Penric, interested. Although now was not the time to follow it up.

"We met once or twice." Also recognizing the diversion, he waved it aside for a much more urgent concern. "You saw where Magal lay? Her soul was not"—he swallowed—"astray or sundered, I trust?"

"Seemingly not."

Hamo's shoulders slumped in relief. "That, at least," he muttered, and tapped his lips in a brief prayer of gratitude to their mutual god.

There followed some time devoted to physical necessities: carrying the sorceress's body to a decent temporary rest in a sort of infirmary at the far end of the house, sending for the female physician Oswyl recommended as working often with his Order's unhappy (Penric read it *gruesome*) inquiries, requisitioning a dedicat to take the locators' horses back to their mews and the carthorse back to its livery. Junior Locator Thala, perhaps expecting to be sent off on this lowly task, brightened at being allowed to stay by Oswyl's side.

They eventually fetched up at what was clearly Hamo's working office on the third floor: crowded shelves, writing table piled high with papers, not quite enough chairs, a lapse Hamo repaired by stealing one from a neighboring chamber.

As soon as they were seated—not settled, Pen gauged *unsettled* was closer to describing the mood in the room—Oswyl began in what must be practiced formality.

"I am sorry for the loss of your colleague—and friend?"

"Both, I hope," said Hamo.

"But I must ask a great many questions."

"Please do," sighed Hamo. "This is…this is horrible. Mags is lying downstairs, while some sundered fool is out there… Whatever you require, Locator." And Pen didn't need second sight to read the sincerity in his voice. Thala removed a little notebook and a lead stylus from her vest, and sat back looking attentive.

"First, I must know Learned Magal's kin. The porter mentioned children?"

"Yes, two, a daughter and a son. Her daughter lately made a very good marriage to a silversmith, and her son is apprenticed to an instrument maker. Both here in Easthome. Oh gods, I must send someone to tell them, or, no, I should go—"

"I will undertake that task next, Learned. It's in my mandate for such tragedies, and such close kin should not be told second-hand."

Hamo looked relieved, and gave up the names and addresses of the two, which the assistant jotted down.

"And a husband?" Oswyl asked. Given that Magal was a member of the Bastard's Order, the presence of children did not necessarily imply the presence of a husband, howsoever it required a father.

Hamo shook his head. "She was widowed a few years ago. Earlier in her career she served as the divine of a temple in Oxmeade"—a large town a half-day's ride from Easthome, Pen recalled—"and he was the long-time choirmaster there. A very devoted couple, from all I've been able to gather. But her single state was one of her many qualities that made her a good candidate to become a sorceress."

"Did the widow have any new suitors? Or, pardon but I must ask, lovers?"

Hamo blinked, perhaps realizing for the first time that the locator was collecting a list of suspects. "None that I know. She did not seem to wish for one."

"Would you know?" asked Oswyl. By sorcerous means, Pen gathered he meant.

"Yes," said Hamo, more certainly. Oswyl cast a look at Pen, who gave him a brief nod.

Penric then offered a question he wasn't sure would occur to Oswyl: "How long ago did she receive her demon?"

"Not long. Just three months. I thought they were settling in so well together." He rubbed his forehead and burst out, "This makes no *sense*. She was levelheaded, amiable, experienced—a decade serving all sorts of people as a temple divine will certainly disclose one's character—are you sure it couldn't have been some terrible accident or mistake?"

"I haven't ruled out anything yet. Not even that."

Penric could almost *see* Oswyl struggling not to say aloud, *But it just doesn't smell right.* The locator had earned Pen's respect last winter. Only now was he beginning to garner Pen's pity as well. Pen was increasingly glad this grim task was Oswyl's calling, and not his own.

Oswyl went on, "Any other kin? Or in-laws?"

"Not here in town. Mags has—had none living, and her late husband's family are all back in Oxmeade."

"Friends and colleagues here in Easthome?"

"Many of both. She was well-liked."

"Any of special note?"

Hamo tossed off a few names, which the assistant dutifully jotted down.

"Were any of these colleagues rival candidates to receive a demon?"

Was Oswyl imagining professional jealousy, to add to jealousy in love? Pen supposed he had to cover every aspect.

"Well, Learned Basum is also waiting for the next opportunity, but I wouldn't call him a rival."

"Why not?"

Pen put in, "Temple demons are almost always handed down to riders of the same sex." At Oswyl's questioning glance, he added, "My case was unusual, as Learned Ruchia had her fatal seizure of the heart unexpectedly, on the road near Greenwell as I was passing by. Her demon was supposed to have been handed off to a female physician-aspirant, waiting at her deathbed."

"And that's another thing," Hamo burst out. "I thought Mags might become my successor, in some few years, and at the end of her life have a demon tamed enough to grant to a physician. It's...the waste goes on and on. Utter *waste*." Hamo increasingly had the look of a man who needed to go apart to cry, or rave, or both, as the enormity of the loss to both himself and the Temple sunk in.

Oswyl, with a list of people to tax growing longer than his arm, looked as though he wanted to let him. But Hamo himself turned to Penric.

"And you found no sign at all of where her demon went?"

The missing demon was as much Hamo's task to manage and regulate as the late woman; in its own way, it, too, had a Temple career. Pen wasn't sure if Oswyl quite grasped this yet, though Inglis, with his experience of Great Beasts cultivated over decades, surely did. Inglis had been very silent throughout this interview, possibly daunted by glimpsing what his own disastrous misadventure must have been like for the people trying to follow after him.

"None, sir," said Pen. "It was very disquieting."

"It could not have got far on its own without seizing on some being of matter to sustain it," said Hamo.

"Yes. A person, either accidently or on purpose, or an animal, likewise—"

"An animal," faltered Hamo, "would have its own dire consequences to such a developed demon."

"Yes, sir, I am very aware. Or the third possibility." They both grimaced.

"Which is what?" prodded Oswyl.

Hamo answered, "If there is no creature whatsoever in range capable of absorbing a demon when its host-creature dies, even a small bird, it...I suppose you could say dissipates. Returns to its elemental chaos, losing all the knowledge it used to hold. Even the ability to be an elemental capable of starting over with the next animal along. Just...gone."

"It sounds a lot like sundering," said Oswyl, his eyes narrowing as he tried to picture this.

"Very like," agreed Pen. "Only faster." Within him, Desdemona shuddered.

Hamo regarded Pen intently. "Did you have any sense of that, in that clearing?"

Pen hesitated. "It's not something I've ever encountered before, so as to immediately recognize some trace." *Nor I,* Des conceded. *Such instances are, by their nature, never witnessed.*

"Our stray demon must be sought, and I can't leave here with all the rites to arrange for Mags," said Hamo, with an agitated swipe of his hand through his hair. "My own people are scattered, or unsuitable." He glanced across at Oswyl, who held up his palms in a fending gesture, and Pen tried unsuccessfully to remember the name of that Easthome sorcerer Oswyl had so definitely clashed with last winter. He, too, must be one of Hamo's flock. Hamo's gaze circled back to Pen. "Learned Penric…"

Penric, seizing the hint, nodded. "I'd be very pleased to assist you in this matter, if I can beg leave of my superior the princess-archdivine." Which he likely could. Inglis shifted, but said nothing. Yet.

Oswyl looked very relieved. "I'd be pleased to accept your assistance." He glanced more hesitantly at Inglis. "And yours, Shaman…?"

"I'd like to take another look at that clearing," said Inglis slowly. "Before it has a chance to rain. There were—I'd just like some more time to cast a wider search." For what, he did not say, but Pen recalled that mysterious third arrow, and the bit of fox-fluff it had caught. And wondered what tracking abilities Inglis's wolf-within might lend him, even beyond the hunting skills of Pen's canton-mountain youth.

"Wherever Magal's demon is now," said Penric, "it had to have started out from that point. We should go together. Tomorrow morning."

"Early," agreed Inglis, earning an approving nod from Oswyl.

Oswyl went on to Hamo, "Does—did—Learned Magal keep a chamber here, or live elsewhere?"

"Yes, she lived in."

"I'll need to look through her things, if you can undertake to keep her room undisturbed till I get back. Probably also tomorrow morning. We must go to the next-of-kin tonight, before it gets any later." He added a bit wearily, "And then report to my own superiors."

Everyone present having a hundred new chores pressing down upon them, Oswyl extracted his party with more condolences, assuring Hamo that this tragedy would have his inquiry office's utmost attention.

BY THE time Pen had made it back to the Temple guest house reserved for the princess-archdivine and her train, hastily washed up, donned his best and cleanest white robes, and dashed down to the courtyard, he was running very late, as well as just running. Well, more of an awkward skipping, as he tried to blend the dignity due from a learned divine with his need for speed. But his superior was still being loaded into her sedan chair when he came puffing up.

"Ah, Penric," she greeted him. "And Desdemona, of course." The smile on her aging lips was dry, but not actually annoyed. "At last. I was preparing to send you to bed without any supper at all, if you missed this one." Llewen kin Stagthorne was dressed tonight as princess and royal aunt, not Temple functionary, though her gown showed off silks of Martensbridge manufacture, one of the more lucrative enterprises of the Daughter's Order that she oversaw there.

"My apologies for my tardiness, Your Grace," he replied, bending to kiss her archdivine's ring held forgivingly out to him. The hand went on to flick at her bearers, who hoisted up her chair and began to cart her along downhill towards Kingstown.

"Walk beside me, then," she said serenely, "and tell me all about your day off. I take it the fish were either very good or very bad?"

"Neither, as it turned out. Locator Oswyl was called out on an inquiry in the early morning—"

"Oh, that's a pity. I know you were looking forward to a visit. I quite liked him, during his brief sojourn in Martensbridge last winter. And your shaman friend was…interesting." She paused to consider this. "So good he wasn't hanged."

"I must agree. It would have been a pointless waste. Among other things. But we spent the day with Oswyl despite all, because he came to ask us both to help with his inquiry. And so some innocent fish were spared."

Her glance aside was sharp. "Really. And thereby hangs a tale?"

"Yes, Your Grace, but not one for the street." The bearers allowed the honor of transporting her, sturdy dedicats in the blue and white of their goddess and hers, were not the only prick-eared listeners within range.

Her eyelids lowered in understanding. "After, then. I am too old to stay out late, even for the sake of my Stagthorne kin."

"And I've undertaken to go out early tomorrow, so our steps will match on that."

"Hm." She digested this, then set aside her curiosity for dessert. "In any case, you will gratify me tonight by introducing yourself as Learned Lord Penric kin Jurald of Martensbridge, instead of your usual contraction."

"Too wordy, Your Grace. It offends my sense of literary economy."

She sniffed. "There are places where a pious humility is a suitable thing. Tonight's venue is not one of them. You are my sorcerer; your status reflects on my own."

His conceding nod was undercut by his grimace. "Jurald Court is little more than a fortified farmhouse in an obscure mountain valley, and I am its portionless younger son, as you and I both know."

"But no one else here will, and you are in no wise obliged to inform them. The world is not always so friendly a place that you can afford to squander your advantages on a pointless conceit."

"I much prefer the meaningful title I earned to the empty one I inherited."

"So, not modesty at all, but sly pride? Your scholarship is a delight to me, Penric, but of the many things you learned in seminary, I doubt court polish was one."

"Recalling our meals in the student refectory, I'm afraid you're right," he granted ruefully.

"Think of this visit as an opportunity for a different kind of learning, then. Another day will put some other plate on your table, more to your taste, but do not waste the food in front of you."

"Yes, Your Grace," he said meekly.

Their conversation broke off as her guards and bearers, and the second sedan chair porting her inseparable secretary, negotiated the long flights of steps crisscrossing down the bluff. Pen fell behind as the lanes narrowed and twisted, then strode up beside Llewen again as they came to the wider street fronted by the mansion of the royal relative hosting tonight's festivities. When the chair grounded beside the entrance, he was granted the privilege of raising her to her silk-slippered feet and offering her his arm, which she took with a rather smug smile.

The official naming ceremony for the blobby scrap of humanity Penric had been assured was a prince had gone off smoothly, the gods be thanked, three days ago. So he supposed the worst was over. Since the Archdivine of Easthome had officiated, Penric was not sure what his own superior's Temple task had been, besides swelling an already impressive procession. Good fairy, perhaps? Penric's function had seemed to be to stand around, look decorative, and try desperately to guard his best white robes against the detritus of a busy city. Tonight was shaping to be a reprise.

He even spotted some of the same faces, here in the hall of the elderly lord who was husband to Llewen's even-more-aged sister Princess Llewanna—Llewen released her hold on Pen to embrace this sibling. Really, it didn't seem all that different from some of the princess-archdivine's god's-day banquets back in Martensbridge. Well, more lords, fewer merchants. Fewer Temple folk, for that matter; Pen didn't spot that many other robes. More highborn relatives, though the influx of the aristocracy into town was already starting to thin. More expensive clothes and jewels. Ambassadors from far countries, not near counties, all right, that was a novelty—perhaps he'd have a chance to practice his languages before the evening was over. Men whose mistakes could kill more people, faster; but still, just men.

The candlelit banquet chamber was excessively warm in the summer evening. Pen sat by Llewen's left hand and was painfully polite to the few people who spoke to him and not her, smiling but not too much, since she'd once chided him for the latter. Was *court polish* a euphemism for being very bored while being stuffed very full?

It wasn't until the tables were being cleared away for the doubtless sedate dancing that he spotted an object of interest, or at least another person under fifty years old. The young fellow was even skinnier than Pen, managing to look less like a lord and more like a very well-dressed scarecrow. His most prominent feature was a pair of the thickest glass spectacles Pen had ever seen on a person's face.

They drifted together next to a wall wainscoted in gilded leather. "Is that not Martensbridge lens-craft?" Pen inquired, as pleased as if he'd run across an unexpected old acquaintance from his home village.

"Ah!" The young man's hand flew to his gold-decked temple. "You know the work?"

"Yes, very well. And the workman, I daresay. The artisan in Lower Linden Street, yes? I've heard several of my more aged colleagues pour blessings upon his head. And his hands."

The fellow's chest swelled as much as it could. "You understand!" He peered more questioningly at Pen. "Do you?"

"As I can think of no greater nightmare than to lose my ability to read, yes."

The bespectacled lordling smiled gratefully. "I was fourteen before I even found mine. Everyone just thought I was a clumsy fool when I was younger."

"Oh, that's unfortunate."

He nodded. "Because I could see shapes and colors and light and movement just fine, I didn't think myself blind, didn't realize others saw so much more than me. And neither did they. It was a Temple divine who'd been trying to tutor me, and who wore them himself, who first suspected my malady, and took me to Martensbridge to have me fitted. It was a revelation. Trees had *leaves*. And letters were not elusive fur-bearing creatures hiding coyly behind each other. I wasn't stupid, I just couldn't *see*." He was a little breathless, getting this all out at once to a rare sympathetic listener.

"When I graduated Rosehall with second honors, it was the proudest day of my life, and no one understood why I was weeping till I nearly couldn't see again. Except Yvaina." He nodded sharply at this mysterious codicil.

"I attended the white god's seminary at Rosehall," Pen returned, quite willing to be cheerful for a fellow bookman's miracle. "I wonder if we could have been there at the same time?" Or not; Pen would certainly have remembered the spectacles, however unprepossessing their owner. Although the great university at Rosehall did host some six thousand students at a time. "I took my braids and oaths a year ago this spring."

"I left four years back," the young man said. "So maybe?"

"Mm, no. That would have been just about the time I arrived."

His brows crimped in puzzlement over the arithmetic; a divine's training normally took six years, not three. But he shrugged this off.

Pen asked, "What was your study?"

"Mathematics, mostly. I'd hoped to find a place in the Father's Order, perhaps rising to comptroller, at which point I thought I could afford to marry.

I even began there as a lay dedicat. But, uh, other things happened first."

A young woman approached them, nearly as lanky and scrawny as the man apart from the distinctive pregnant bulge about her middle, like a plum on a stick. Pen had thought Des had fallen asleep, as he'd wished he could do, but she put in, *The word you are groping for, young Pen, is* willowy. *Far more flattering, thus safer. Trust me.*

Her clothes, though rich, hung on her almost as tentatively as the fellow's, but at the sight of her his face lit as though the sun had come out behind his winking lenses.

"Ah. Allow me to introduce my wife. Baroness Yvaina kin Pikepool. And, oh, you are, learned sir...?"

Pikepool was not one of the major Wealdean kin houses, or Llewen would have made Pen con it before now. Possibly not as obscure, however, as his own. Pen bowed. "Lord Penric kin Jurald, presently of Martensbridge."

"Ah, that's why you were sitting with the Princess Llewen at the high table. You looked a very daunting guardian."

Yvaina's rather thick brows knotted. "Is that not a Darthacan name?"

"Saonese, courtesy of a younger son with a short-lived dower and a last canton kin land-heiress. Then you would be Baron...?"

The fellow opened his hands as if in embarrassment. "Wegae kin Pikepool. Though only lord for the last two years. The inheritance was quite unexpected."

The name might be obscure, but it was memorable. "You wouldn't happen to own a large tract of wooded hills about ten miles east of here?"

Wegae blinked in surprise. "It's part of the old family seat. That and that dreadful falling-down fortress. It's only good for a hunting lodge anymore, if I had the least interest in hunting." He made an excusing gesture at his face. "That was another skill no one could beat into me as a lad, along with reading."

He had not betrayed the slightest flinch at the question. Possibly no one had informed him yet of what had been found this morning in his woods? Oswyl, with all those closer relatives and colleagues of Magal's to work through, might not get to him till tomorrow. Pen decided he'd better not step on the locator's lines, contenting himself with, "Very pretty countryside."

Wegae shrugged. "We prefer the house in town, traitorous to my forest-tribe ancestors though it may be to admit it." His lady smiled and wrapped his arm in hers, comfortingly.

Penric tried to think of a subtle way to ask, *Where were you last night?* "Have you been much taken up with this royal launching?" A circling hand-wave indicated the past two weeks of name-day festivities.

Wegae shook his head. "Only to route around, mostly. But my mother insisted we come tonight. I think my inheritance gratified her almost more than me."

"Well, mothers," Penric offered in prudently vague sympathy. Both his auditors nodded in unison.

The princess-archdivine's lady secretary found Pen then, to murmur, "Her Grace is ready to leave now."

Pen was forced to make polite introductions and farewells in the same breath. He let the secretary guide him past the hazards of thanks to their highborn hosts, and, safely outside, took his place beside the sedan chair once more. Uphill, there was less breath for gossip, at least on his part, and the same problem with listening ears. So it wasn't until Llewen invited him to her rooms that, seated between the two women in the candlelight, he was able to recount his day's experiences. Despite his weariness, he tried to make it all sound as interesting as possible.

He must have succeeded, for his superior finally said, mildly, "I did have other plans for you tomorrow."

Did have not *do*, right. "So did I, Your Grace"—though probably not the same ones—"but I'd like to help Oswyl find justice for that poor sorceress if I can. And no one else is speaking for the lost demon. It was a victim, too, in my view."

She gave a conceding wave of her beringed hand. "Report to me again tomorrow night, then."

Playing on her curiosity had worked, good. Relieved, he signed himself, managed not to yawn in her face, and made his way to his own chamber.

BY THE time Penric and Inglis rode out from Easthome at dawn, made arrangements to leave their horses in the hill-village temple's paddock, discouraged the lay dedicat from tagging along, and returned to the clearing, it was not as early as either had hoped. At least the light was good.

Beginning from the dried blood patch, infested now by only a few green flies, Penric walked out in a slow spiral, all his senses deployed. No ghosts today, either, and at length he conceded that any chill of unease was being supplied by his own imagination.

Inglis went off to look for telltale horse droppings or cart tracks, and found some, but, given all the animals and people that had been in and out of here yesterday, they failed to be definitive. Yet another search for where the bowman must have stood to make his killing shots found no special clues. Inglis came back to the center of the clearing, held out an arm toward the stream, and squinted along it. "He shot the woman from somewhere in that arc of woods. But he shot at the fox from here near the body."

"If the body was even there yet. I'll grant you the shot."

Inglis shrugged and led some forty paces through the brush to the spot where he'd found the third arrow. The gouge in the ground where it had landed was barely visible. No sign of blood or the struggles of a dying animal.

"Can you, ah, smell a trail?" Pen asked him.

"Not exactly. My nose is no keener than any man's. It's just something I attend to more closely."

As his second sight was granting him nothing, Pen was content to follow Inglis's first nose. They wandered generally toward the hidden stream, eyes on the ground. The shaman, too, had hunted in his youth; the Raven Range from which his kin hailed was not as breathlessly high as the mountains in the cantons, but they'd been rugged enough. So Pen was not too surprised when Inglis stopped at the streambank, pointed down, and said "Ah," in a tone of satisfaction.

Fox prints dappled the mud, though only a few. More useful were a couple of human dents, one of which lay half-atop a pawprint, plus a deep round pock that might have been from a walking stick. "Someone gave chase. Or tracked," said Inglis.

Pen tried matching the prints with his own, off to the side, and examined the results. The original footprint was a touch longer, quite a bit wider, and deeper. "Long stride, or running. A heavier man than me."

"Most men are, surely." But Inglis made a similar test on the other side, and allowed, "Heavier than me, as well."

"The arrow was undamaged, but he didn't stop to pick it up," Pen noted.

"Might have been dark by then."

"Not so dark he didn't take a long shot at a fast-moving fox. And nearly hit it."

"Hm."

They picked up the tracks on the other side of the stream. The fox's were quickly lost, the man's soon after, although a few broken branches or ambiguous scrapes in the soil led them onward. After about two miles of thrashing through the steep and treacherous undergrowth, Inglis, huffing, plunked down on a fallen log and said, "That's it for me."

Penric joined him, catching his breath and staring around. This tract measured some six or seven miles on a side, giving something like forty or fifty square miles of precipitous green woods. They needed a better plan than blundering around at random.

Inglis scratched his sweating chin. "So, I gather you are thinking this fox might have picked up your missing demon?"

Penric opened his hands in doubt. "Not an impossibility. Although any human, no matter how unsavory, would have been a first choice for it. A fox before a bird or squirrel, though."

"You once told me that demons always try to jump higher, to a larger or more powerful animal, or person to a more powerful person."

"If they can."

"What happens if one can't? If it is forced downward?"

Penric sighed. "What do you think would happen to you, if someone tried to force your body into a box half its size?"

Inglis's brows twitched up. "Nothing very pleasant. Crushed, I suppose. Maybe bits cut off."

"Something like that, I gather. Except happening to a mind instead of a body."

"But a demon isn't a material thing. Shouldn't it be more…foldable?"

" 'Spirit cannot exist in the world without matter to sustain it,' " Penric quoted. "Maybe it's more like…being forced to exist on half the food and water and air you require. Or a shrub transplanted with nine-tenths of its roots amputated. Or I-don't-know what material metaphor. But this demon, if I understand Hamo aright, contained imprints of at least three human minds and lives including, now, Magal's, together with any animals that went before. That's not a small demon."

"So…somewhere out there is a very smart fox?" He added meticulously, "Assuming the fox."

"Smart, mentally mutilated, and insane. Or worse."

"Wait. The woman who was murdered is now in the fox?" Inglis considered this. "You might want to add *angry* to that list."

"Angry, bewildered, terrified, the Bastard knows what." Well, He probably did, at that. Pen hoped the soul of Magal had found deep comfort in His care. The image of Magal...required another caretaker. And Penric was horribly afraid he could guess just who the god had tapped for the task.

Time to earn your keep, O Learned Divine? said Des, amused. *As I recall the Saint of Idau once gave us a warning about that.*

Mm. Pen sighed, not happily. *Any suggestions, Des?*

An impression of a shrug. *Such manly sports as fox hunts were never ours. Well, Aulia hawked as a girl in Brajar. Sugane set snares, though her most notable weapon was a rusty spear. Rogaska killed more chickens than any fox, but she didn't need to hunt them farther than her father's farmyard. Still...* She turned Pen's head. *Try over that way.*

"Let's take a cast up there." Pen pointed, and with a shrug Inglis rose to follow him. They pulled their way upslope from sapling to sapling, then came out onto a stretch of flatter, less obstructed ground.

Penric, for a moment, tried to control his busy mind and just let himself drift, or be drawn.

"Oh," said Inglis, and his stride lengthened. After a few more paces Pen could hear it too, a muffled whine.

Near the base of an oak tree, they found the pit-trap, sprung and occupied. Inglis knelt to clear away the disordered concealing branches, and they both peered down. A smell of dubious fish, elderly pork fat, and the sharp reek of fox wafted out to greet them. The trap's resident cowered and bared its teeth up at them, growling.

"A fox," said Pen, "but not our fox."

"I can sense that. Hm."

The pit did not seem to be freshly dug, but it had been freshly straightened and, of course, freshly baited. And not, evidently, with poisoned bait.

"Why trap a fox alive?" Pen mused.

"Keeping the pelt intact?"

"Fall or winter is the season for good pelts."

"Any season will do for farmers warring on vermin," Inglis noted.

"Then why not use a snare or an iron trap?"

They both stood back and frowned down at this new puzzle.

"Hoy! You there!" a brusque voice yelled.

Pen's gaze jerked up to find a man in hunts-man's leathers approaching them, his bow drawn. He scowled more fiercely than the fox. But he hesitated as his auditors failed to run away like surprised poachers.

Despite this check, he gathered his resolve and went on, "What are you doing trespassing on Pikepool lands? I'll see you off!"

Penric, his eyes on the bent bow and trying to make out the fletching on the nocked arrow, scrambled over the blank in his mind and came out with, "Ah, you must be Baron kin Pikepool's forester! I met Wegae and his willowy wife last night at Princess Llewanna's dinner. He recommended his woods to my attention. Permit me to introduce myself." Penric managed a short, polite nod, aristocrat to servant. "Lord Penric kin Jurald." He elbowed Inglis.

"Inglis kin Wolfcliff," Inglis came through, though he cast Pen an eyebrow-lift. That high kin name, certainly, would be recognized by any Wealding. Pen let the notion that they were here by some lordly invitation stand implied.

"Aye..." The bow lowered, thankfully, although the suspicious glower remained. Arrows that he could see *coming* were no threat to a sorcerer, but Pen decided he'd rather not reveal his calling just yet. "I'm the baron's man."

"Oh, very good!" said Penric, with a cheer he hoped did not sound too desperate. "Then you can tell us about this trap."

The man stared at him anew. "It's a pit trap. As any foo—man can see."

"I see, well, smell you baited it for foxes. Got one, too, very good."

"Aye...?"

"Have foxes been a particular problem around here lately?"

"Vermin's always a problem." Slowly, the man eased the bowstring, un-nocked his arrow, and returned it to his quiver. "We clear them out from time to time."

Penric smiled and rubbed his neck. "How many foxes might live in these woods, d'you think, Inglis?"

By his expression, Inglis was not following this start, but he shrugged. "You might find one to three on a square mile, usually, for land like this. More this time of year, when the new pups take to the field."

"So...anywhere from fifty to a couple of hundred? My word. That's a lot of foxes," Pen marveled, trying for an air of city enthusiasm. The bowman winced, though whether at Pen's tone or his arithmetic was unclear. "I had no idea. You certainly have your work cut out for you, forester! And what would your name be?"

The man gave it up reluctantly: "Treuch."

Penric backed up from the pit and waved as though inviting the man to partake of a repast. "Well, don't let us impede your work. Carry on, Treuch!"

On the way, Pen managed a closer look at the fletching bristling from the quiver. Similar to the arrows they'd found yesterday, but not obviously identical. Unhelpful.

Do you make anything of him, Des?

Seems very tense. But he would be, encountering trespassers who outnumber him, and younger men at that.

Treuch might be any age from his mid-thirties to his mid-forties—a forester's life was no easy one. He seemed about Inglis's height and weight, if more bowed. But he donned a pair of thick leather gauntlets and lowered himself into the pit with considerable agility, first trapping the animal between his knees and muzzling its bite with a swift wrapping of rawhide cord, then binding its feet and lifting it out. Inglis, unasked, bent to help in this task. The fox, which had snarled at the huntsman, shrank from the wolf-shaman and whimpered.

Treuch managed a gruff, "Thankee," as he clambered back out. He rebaited the trap with some offal from his pack, then arranged the concealing branches and leaves once more. Slinging the squirming animal over his shoulder, he stood and regarded his unwanted visitors.

"Best you see yourselves out of the woods, and watch your step when you do. I've some snares set about as well. But Dorra, the alewife up at Weir village, makes a good brew. If you go out that way, likely you can quench a gentlemanly thirst there speedily enough."

"Good advice," said Pen, "on both counts. Shall we wend our way to Dorra, Inglis?"

"If you say so," said Inglis.

"Good hunting," Pen called over his shoulder as they tromped off in the opposite direction to the fox-burdened forester.

They kept walking, carefully, only until the man was out of earshot before stopping in mutual accord.

"You want to follow that fellow?" asked Inglis quietly.

"Absolutely."

They turned and retraced their steps, much more silently.

Treuch made his way through more of the track-less stretch, then turned onto a trail and strode faster. Penric and Inglis kept just out of sight behind him, although they almost came to grief when he turned aside to check a snare. They hunkered down until he returned to the path. After about two miles, he came to an open area. Pen and Inglis stopped at the shaded verge, concealing themselves in an overgrown copse.

An old stone building, half castle, half farm-house, rose tall and brown on the far side of the wide cleared area. Some thatch-roofed houses of wattle-and-daub in various states of disrepair clustered at its feet, along with a stable set in an L around its own courtyard. Wood fences pastured a pair of oxen and a few horses. A better-mended fence set off a large kitchen garden.

The forester disappeared around the side of the stable, then returned in a few minutes, foxless. He trudged off to the stone house and let himself in through a heavy oak door. The yard fell silent.

The sheer face of the manor house boasted very few eyes, its windows small, deep set, and, as nearly as Pen could tell at this distance, very dirty. "Do you sense anyone else about?"

Inglis nodded toward a chimney in one of the daub houses, venting smoke from a cooking fire. "Likely people in there."

"Hm. Well, they'll be busy about their tasks. Let's see what he did with that fox."

Inglis shrugged but followed behind Penric, his curiosity, too, overcoming his prudence.

The stable had once been meant for more horses, judging by the number and generous proportions of the stalls. All its current residents seemed to be out in the pasture, leaving several doors hanging open or half open. Only one stall had both the top and bottom halves of its door latched.

Gently, trying to make no squeak, Pen unlatched the top and swung it part open. He blinked to try to adjust his eyes to the shadows, then gave up and thought, *Des, light.*

Some half-a-dozen, no, seven unhappy foxes were imprisoned within. Some lay in the straw panting in apparent exhaustion, others crouched as far from their fellows as they could get, growling.

Several were bleeding from fox fights. The hostile atmosphere, Pen thought, was much the same as one might get by jamming seven sorcerers and their demons into a similar space.

"That," Inglis muttered, "is a decidedly odd thing to do with foxes."

"Really. If that fellow spoke the truth about thinning the local vermin, they should all be pelts tacked to the stable wall by now, waiting for the women servants to get around to scraping them."

"So what's next? I might add, my probationary status with the Fellowship would not be helped by my being either arrested for trespassing, or for getting into a fight trying to avoid being arrested for trespassing."

"Yet...hm. You have a valid point. We need Oswyl up here in order to go much further."

"For what? It's not against the law to trap foxes. Especially by a forester on his own lord's land."

"All right. That's a problem, too." Convincing the somewhat rigid Oswyl of...what? Even Pen wasn't sure.

Inglis snorted softly. "It does look like, if you were craving to survey all the foxes on this land, someone seems to be doing it for you. Might be easier to stand off and wait."

"Except there is one fox out there I'd rather no one catch but me."

"I wonder if anyone *could* catch it but you?"

"Hm." Which led directly to the uncomfortable question of the state of mind of the lost demon, trapped in a lower animal that could not support it. It might (if indeed in a fox, not yet proved) make a very shrewd fox indeed. Or it might make for a drowning agony of confusion and despair. Easily mistaken for a sick fox by anyone, and thereby hung a whole host of other hazards.

"I'd want to find out what Oswyl has uncovered today, first," said Inglis. "Before..."

He didn't complete the thought, but the heartening implication seemed to be that if Pen wanted to try something chancy in aid of all this, he might not have to do it alone. Pen bit his lip, trying to think. They were supposed to meet Oswyl in town for dinner, and there relate the events of each of their days. The light was leveling. By the time they made it back to the hill village of Weir, collected their horses, and rode down into Easthome, it would be well on toward evening.

"I think," said Pen slowly, "we'd better withdraw for tonight, before someone catches us skulking around. Come back tomorrow in better force."

Inglis nodded agreement, and they turned to slip away into the woods. At the last moment Pen stepped back, unlatched the lower door to the stall, and edged it open. Inglis raised his brows but did not comment until they had reached the cover of the copse once more. As they paused to look back, they saw one rusty streak, then another, flit around the corner of the stable and speed for the forest.

"Two hundred foxes," Inglis murmured. "Do you think your god has His thumb in all this?"

"Oh, yes," sighed Pen, signed himself, and tapped his lips twice.

THE TAVERN where they were to rendezvous was a modest place, tucked up in an alley not far from the big chapterhouse of the Father's Order on the Templetown heights. They found Oswyl and his assistant arrived before them, though not by much, in a small upstairs chamber, a compromise between cheap and private. But the pitcher of beer the servant brought was decent, the tureen of stew contained identifiable meat, the bread and butter were abundant, and Penric, by this time, was starving. The servant's presence gave them all a welcome head start on the meal, but at last he decamped, closing the door behind him.

Though town-clean, Oswyl looked even more tired than Pen felt after barging around in the woods all day. Both Oswyl and his assistant Thala, who Penric gathered was also his apprentice, were dressed in their most formal gray uniforms, having just come from Learned Magal's funeral; it being high summer, the ceremony had not been delayed. Penric was relieved to learn that the Easthome sacred animals had plainly signed her soul as taken up by the white god.

"Her service was very well attended," Thala remarked. "Whoever killed her either did not know or did not care how much his deed would have her entire Easthome Order up in arms against him."

"Aye," said Oswyl. "Although I spoke to as many as I could, and their most common response after anger was bewilderment. Kin and colleagues both. Usually by this time in an inquiry I start to have some direction, some odd crack, some... unpleasant smell, but not here. She seems to have been the most blameless woman imaginable. I'd feel myself forced back to *shot by mistake for a deer*, except no one had any idea what she was doing out in those woods in the first place. Either she'd told no one of her errand, or at least one person was lying to me." He sighed, as if this latter were an irreducible hazard.

"We made a good start on finding out everything she'd done day before yesterday," said Thala, "right down to what she ate for breakfast, but about the third hour of the afternoon she left the chapterhouse and just never came back."

"Afoot?" said Inglis. "Hard to get all the way up to those woods before dark that way. Livery stables...?"

"We're in process of canvassing them all," said Oswyl. "No luck yet."

"Why shoot a sorceress?" Pen mused. "Why murder anyone, for that matter?" Belatedly self-conscious, he managed not to glance at Inglis. "I mean, in a premeditated way."

Oswyl chased a bite of bread with a long swallow of beer, then sat back. "Some reasons are more common than others."

"Money?" asked Inglis. "An inheritance...?"

"Money to be sure, but inheritances very rarely. Usually murder happens in the course of a robbery. Next most common is some brawl or ambush after losses at play, and after that, debt."

"Her purse was still tied to her belt," observed Thala, "though it didn't hold much, and those little pearl earrings were still in her ears. No ordinary cutpurse would have left either. Stolen demons I can't speak to."

Oswyl nodded at her in a mentor's approval. "Magal was an orphan, she didn't gamble, and she neither owed nor was owed money," he said. "We've checked all that. She owned no property. What she inherited from her late husband went to her daughter's dowry and her son's apprenticeship."

"Temple divines are seldom rich," Penric noted.

"To hear them complain of it, no, yet they seldom go hungry," said Oswyl. Penric considered his dinner of last night, and let this comment go by. Oswyl continued, "But no, I'm...let's say I would be surprised if money turns out to be an issue in this.

"Then there's jealousy. And not just rivalries of the bedchamber, in all their customary variations. Siblings. Colleagues, fellow workmen, fellow students. The envy by one with lesser skill or luck of those with greater. Some very corrosive emotions, there. Except I've found nothing of that sort hanging on Learned Magal's robes, either. So far." He drank again, and frowned. "An odd sort of fellow traveler with jealousy and envy is revenge. That one can be tricky. People, and not just the stupid sort, can decide that the most absurd things were an unbearable slight to them. And not necessarily in retaliation for some wrongdoing, or in some cases even right-doing, as we of the Father's Order have sometimes suffered." He grimaced in memory. "Not all who experience justice appreciate it."

"That has possibilities," said Penric. "A sorcerer might easily perform some legitimate act in service of their duties to which some caught-out wrongdoer might take exception. The person to ask in that case would be Learned Hamo."

"If it were obvious, I'd think he should have thought of it sooner than this, and volunteered the information," said Oswyl. "Nonetheless, yes, it does seem worth asking again." He sopped up the last of his stew with a morsel of bread. "So much for our day in town." As exhausting as it had been fruitless, apparently. "What of yours in the woods?"

Penric and Inglis took turns recounting their tale. Oswyl listened intently, his scowl set, till Penric came to his theory of the two hundred foxes, whereupon he looked deeply pained.

Inglis chewed on his knuckle for a moment. "Regarding the fox problem, Pen. I think I might get us some help with that."

"Help how? Ordinary searchers won't be able to tell one fox from another."

"I wasn't thinking of ordinary searchers. But I'll have to ask around before I can make any promises. I'll see what I can find tonight, after this."

Penric wasn't used to thinking of help in Temple matters, given both the solitary nature of demons and the rarity of sorcerers. He wasn't sure whether to give credence to Inglis's words or not, but decided it would be premature to melt with relief.

"Oh," said Penric, "I should add, I met Baron kin Pikepool last night. He and his wife were at a dinner at Princess Llewanna's town mansion."

Oswyl's brows climbed. "Rarified company."

Penric, who had not found it to be all that rarified, shrugged. "He didn't seem to have heard of the murder on his land yet, and I didn't say anything about it. Is he on your list of people to talk to?"

"Very much so. Today, by preference, except that the funeral ran long and I am almost out of today. What did you make of him?"

Penric wondered if he meant, as a suspect? "Young. Bookish. Interesting for that."

"Many men of his rank are skillful sportsmen."

"Not him—bad eyes. Apparently a lifelong affliction. If you are looking for a bowman, he's not it." Not that kin Pikepool couldn't have hired such a mercenary, and easier than most, if his purse was as deep as it had appeared. But why?

Around a last bite, Thala put in, "I was able to speak briefly with one of the kin Pikepool maid-servants this morning. She said her lord spent day-before-yesterday at home, and he and his lady wife had friends in for dinner, who stayed late." She mopped her lips, thoughtfully. "He sounded an unexceptionable employer, if not lordly enough to suit some in his household. The main objection seems to be that he routinely feeds a pack of poor hangers-on from his university days."

Which sounded more like people Pen would care to meet than most of last night's company.

"It would be an odd plan," said Inglis, "for a calculating murderer to leave the body to be found on his own land." He hesitated. "Unless it was someone trying to cast suspicion in kin Pikepool's direction."

"More likely," said Oswyl, "is that the body was intended to be better concealed, but that the murderer didn't get back to do so before it was discovered."

"Because he suddenly decided to chase a fox? Through those dire woods, at night? All night?" said Penric. "That's a very distractible murderer. Or a very important fox."

"You are thinking it bore away Magal's demon, yes? And her murderer knew it?" said Oswyl. "It may be so, but why give chase? If it is as you describe, the demon would be crippled, impotent. And, certainly, unable to accuse her killer."

"Which brings me back to the question, why was the kin Pikepool forester hunting foxes today?" said Penric. "And taking care to catch them alive, which is not the usual approach to foxes."

Oswyl sighed. "So I will add the kin Pikepool forester to my list. After the baron."

"Please." Penric nodded. "He might have been physically capable of the act. Still leaves the problem of why."

Oswyl drummed his fingers on the table and frowned. Some more. "This is not the first time that kin Pikepool has come to the attention of justice in Easthome. But I'm not seeing a connection."

"Oh?" said Penric, trying, and failing, to imagine how Wegae and his willowy spouse could possibly have done so. "Was he caught stealing books?"

Oswyl blinked, then said, "Oh. Not the present baron. His predecessor. Uncle, I think. He was accused of pushing his wife down the stairs during some marital spat. Broke her neck in the fall. Two, three years ago. The tribunal was truncated when the accused man fled the realm. But after some legal delays, his title and property were sequestered for the crime, and passed along to the nephew. I suppose they couldn't leave the estate without management. I don't remember if the old baron was rumored to have died abroad. This is hearsay, by the way. I didn't work on the case— given the status of those involved, it was too far above my head."

"I don't suppose this uncle was a burly bowman?"

"No idea. But that he's a thousand miles away, or dead, and has no known history with Learned Magal whatsoever, disinclines me to get too excited."

"That first could be reversed," noted Inglis. "Not the second, I grant."

"Mm." Oswyl glanced across at Penric. "Would you be willing to come along with me to kin Pikepool tonight? I should like to borrow your rank."

"Which one?" said Penric. "Learned divine? Sorcerer?"

"Those as well, but I was thinking of your kin rank. That is"—Oswyl cleared his throat—"you once told me your father was a baron, Penric, but you had not mentioned whether your mother was a baron's wife."

Irregular birth was a common assumption about members of the Bastard's Order, and too often correct for Penric to take offense. "Very much so, although she's a baron's widow now. There were seven of us, my three sisters and three brothers. And then me, the youngest."

Oswyl nodded. "It will serve to get us in the front door. And not the servants' entrance. Kin lords can be, mm, difficult to deal with to those not of the highest echelon of Temple inquirers, themselves with kin bonds."

"I'd have thought your Temple calling was a password for every portal."

"Unfortunately not." Oswyl paused, eyes narrowing in curiosity. "Why, is yours?"

Penric had never thought about it. "I've...not tried every portal yet."

Oswyl snorted, and rose. "Well, let us see how you work to open this one."

THE KIN Pikepool townhouse lay farther out from the Hallow King's Hall than the lordly mansion of last night, on a narrower street. The row of dwellings was more modest but more recently built, also of the cut stone so common in the capital replacing, by fire and fiat, so many earlier wooden structures. The young baron was evidently sociable enough to keep two cressets bracketing his entry burning in the early night, with a porter to tend them and the door.

"Learned Lord Penric kin Jurald of Martensbridge to see Baron kin Pikepool, upon an urgent Temple matter," Penric told this functionary, thinking of his princess-archdivine's tutorials. "And colleagues." Alas that he hadn't had time to return to his room and change into his whites with his shoulder braids, which spoke so firmly for him. But the porter, after a wary glance at his grubby person and the tidier Grayjays, gave way at least to the point of leaving them standing in the hall rather than on the step while he went to find out if his master was receiving such odd company. He disappeared into a doorway off the single central hallway, returning soon after.

"This way, Learned," and, entering before them, "Learned Lord Penric, my lord. And party."

They entered a pleasant bookroom, primarily furnished with a writing desk behind which their host-and-quarry sat with papers and ledgers spread out. Oil lamps and wall sconces relieved the evening shadows, warming the room quite enough without a fire in the grate. Wegae's eyes, magnified by his spectacles, widened with interest at the pair Penric trailed. "Ah, yes. It's all right, Jons." He unfolded from his chair and came around his desk, receiving Penric standing, as an equal.

Pen ran through the introductions, with no reaction from Wegae beyond baffled curiosity. They were invited to two cushion-padded benches set across from each other before the dark fireplace. The porter brought around the desk chair to make up the numbers, which Wegae took. Penric politely declined Wegae's offer of refreshments, and the servant went off. Penric and Oswyl glanced across at each other. When Oswyl did not at once take the lead, Penric opened his hand to him; he seemed to take a breath like a swimmer before plunging in.

"Yesterday morning, the lay dedicat from the village temple at Weir was checking snares in your woods nearby, when he came across the body of a woman," Oswyl began. "His divine sent promptly to the Father's Order. I was dispatched to examine the scene, together with, later, Learned Penric and Shaman Inglis."

"Five gods," said Wegae, and signed himself in reflexive dismay. "Who was she? What had happened to her?"

Oswyl's narrow look at this first reaction evidently found nothing to pause for—Pen wasn't sure if he was disappointed—for he went on to summarize the scene much as he had for Learned Hamo. "She proved to be an Easthome Temple sorceress, Learned Magal. Do you know the woman? Ever meet or see her?"

Wegae, wide-eyed, shook his head from side to side. "I direct my devotions to the Father's Order these days. I've not had much to do with the house of the white god. They'd always seemed rather strange and secretive, over there. Um." He looked briefly as if he'd like to swallow back that last remark, considering present company, but it was too late and he forged on. "I'd not even met a sorcerer to talk to before Learned Lord Penric last night. Wait." He blinked, turning his head to Pen. "Did you know about this then? Is that why you spoke to me?"

There seemed no reason to dissimulate. "Yes, and yes."

"Why didn't you say anything?"

"At Princess Llewanna's party?" Pen countered, dodging the question nimbly.

Wegae seemed to accept this: "Oh, of course." He scrubbed his hand through his hair, but his stare at Pen remained round. Maybe it was just the spectacles? "Why would anyone do such a heinous thing?"

"That is my puzzle to solve," said Oswyl, "and it's proving peculiar. How she was killed was clear enough. Why is still unknown. It was not theft. The only treasure she bore was her Temple demon, which seems to have, ah, escaped. Perhaps you could speak to that, Penric?"

Penric cleared his throat. "Our present best guess was that when Magal died, her demon jumped to a passing fox, which ran off into your woods. The murderer seems to have given it chase, futilely. Learned Hamo, Magal's Temple superior, has passed me the mandate to locate and secure the lost demon, which we think is still somewhere on your lands."

"Oh," said Wegae. "Did you wish permission to search my woods? Certainly you may."

"Thank you," said Penric, wondering if this was an opportune opening for a confession. *If you're going to, yes*, opined Des. Ah, so she was listening in, good. "In fact, Shaman Inglis and I took a preliminary look up that way earlier today."

"What did you find?" Wegae asked, his interest in the tragedy clearly overshadowing any concern about trespassers on land he never visited. He could have chosen to be sticky about that.

"Not the fox we were looking for, unfortunately. But we did encounter your forester, Treuch, who was very busy about the woods—trapping foxes. He'd secured seven of them alive, so far. I will say, he did his job for you by inviting us to leave."

"Treuch." Wegae grimaced. "He quite frightened me as a boy, when I was dragged up there to try to teach me the sports of a nobleman. I was only my uncle's heir presumptive at that point, his poor wife not yet having proved barren, so eventually my complete ineptitude frustrated them into desisting. Thankfully."

"You could dismiss him now, if you don't like him," Pen noted.

"Oh, I couldn't do that! He's been a kin Pikepool retainer for ages and ages. He knows no other life."

"But you may see," said Oswyl, "why I also wish to obtain your permission to question your people."

"Oh," said Wegae again, more thoughtfully. "Do you think Treuch could have had something to do with it? I mean, he's a hardy man, but he's not...I could picture him killing someone in a drunken brawl, except that he doesn't brawl. Or drink that much."

"Either he has something to do, or knows something about it," suggested Oswyl.

Pen considered yet again his theory of a man killing a woman by mistake for a deer. "If he shot someone in error, thinking them an animal or a poacher, would he run off, or report it?"

"I should think report it, although...a Temple sorceress would be a very alarming victim for the man." He added after a moment, "For any man."

"Do you think he would be physically capable of such an act? Putting two arrows through a person at that distance?" asked Oswyl.

"Well, yes, but..." Wegae shrugged unhappily. "Many men might have that skill. My late uncle, for one."

And himself, for another, Pen reflected. *Could* wasn't *would*. *Necessary but not sufficient*, as his mentors had tagged arguments in seminary.

Wegae went on, "Uncle Halber was a passionate hunter, and skilled in all the usual manly sports. Riding, wrestling, you name it."

"What exactly happened to him?" asked Oswyl.

Wegae looked surprised. "Do you not know? I thought everybody did."

"Only in broad outline. His was not my case, and those inquirers and justiciars most closely involved were obliged not to gossip about it."

Bet they do anyway, murmured Des, *in the halls of their house. Even the Father's devotees are not so inhumanly rigid.*

Hsh, thought Pen back, though he privately agreed.

"I'm not sure I know that much more myself," said Wegae. "I was working as a lay dedicat for the

Father's Order at Shallowford at the time, and only had letters from my mother and sister about the matter, and from the lawyers, until the legal issues were settled and I was sent for. My mother was following things more closely here in Easthome, on my behalf. You might ask her. It was all so very disturbing. Although it did involve a Temple sorceress, come to think."

"Who?" Oswyl and Penric both asked at once.

"Not Magal. What was her name?" He knuckled his forehead. "Sverda. Or Svedra, one of those."

Pen came off-point, letting his breath back out. "Locator Oswyl has likely heard more of the tale than I have. Could you begin at the beginning?"

"Insofar as I know it. My aunt was found dead at the bottom of the main staircase of the old manor house, assumed to have broken her neck in an accidental fall, unwitnessed. It would have passed quietly as a private tragedy, but at her funeral no sacred animal signed her soul as taken up. At my mother's insistence, a Temple sensitive was dispatched at once to look for her ghost, lest her soul be sundered. That was this Learned, um, Svedra. She testified to have found my aunt's shade, repeatedly acting out a different tale on the stairs. She would have it that she was pushed down by her husband, presumably in the midst of one of their many disputes—I have to admit, she was a notable shrew—"

"Not normally a capital crime," Thala muttered almost inaudibly into her notebook, where she'd been industriously jotting.

"Although any woman married to my uncle, well, never mind. And then, apparently, he descended after her to twist her neck to be sure. It might have started as an accident, but it didn't seem to have finished as one, or so it was charged. Anyway, Uncle Halber was arrested on the suspicion, and somewhere in the proceedings seems to have gone over the line from protests to self-justifications. Confession of a sort, I suppose, although not repentance."

"What happened to your aunt?" asked Penric. "Was she sundered?"

"At the very last, no. She'd resisted the prayers performed at the stairs to send her on her way until her husband was finally arrested, but then she consented to go to her goddess. The Daughter, in the end, by her second rites. I hope she found some comfort there. She'd had little enough in life."

The assistant glanced up from her notebook, and asked curiously, "Can ghosts lie?"

Oswyl gave her query an approving nod. "I would never take such testimony as definitive on its own without some cross-check. Or several cross-checks, by preference. At most, it is a pointer, one more scent to follow up."

Good question, Des, Pen thought. Can *ghosts lie?*

Well, they're not usually any smarter *than they were in life... Although they can be mistaken, or still in the grip of the passions that are forcing them to linger. Your friend Oswyl is wise not to take them at face value. As their sundering proceeds, all that fades away, of course.*

"The whole case drew in any number of inquirers and divines and lawyers and judges before it was done," Wegae allowed, "because of my uncle's status. If there was any stone left unturned, it wasn't for lack of trying. I was surprised there was any of the estate left by the time they were all done."

Oswyl dipped his chin in rueful understanding of this.

"How did he come to escape?" asked Pen.

"He was too lightly guarded, I suppose. He was being kept at Magpie House, not the municipal prison, although he was supposed to be moved there once he was sentenced. He must have had help, and a horse, from somewhere."

"How do you know he's dead?" asked Oswyl.

"We had a letter from some mercenary captain in Ibra, addressed to kin Pikepool generally in Easthome, a sort of to-whom-it-may-concern missive—I suspect those captains have practice at the task."

The news about Penric's brother Drovo dying in that mercenary camp in Adria had come from such a captain, although additionally from a friend, Pen was reminded.

"Could it have been forged?" asked Oswyl.

"I've no idea, really." Wegae paused in brief reflection. "On the whole, I hope not. We gave it to the lawyer to keep with the other estate documents—he should still have it, if you wish to examine it."

"Maybe later," said Oswyl, "should it prove in any way pertinent. We've more immediate concerns. May we go up on your lands tomorrow?"

"Yes, certainly. Would you like me to go with you, to smooth things over? The people there don't take well to city strangers, and it's been too long since I visited. I'm supposed to be overseeing it responsibly. The lawyers were very firm on that point." He pushed up his spectacles and vented a small sigh. "The old manor neither produces nor consumes much, but it can't be farmed, the timber is hard to extract, and it has no known minerals. I suppose a hunting preserve remains its best use."

"That might be helpful," allowed Oswyl.

They spent a few minutes arranging a rendezvous for the expedition in the early morning. Wegae himself saw his three visitors to his door, student fashion. Penric wondered if he had not grasped, or just didn't believe in, the much stiffer public manners of most older men of his rank. (The private manners of barons Penric had no illusions about.) Oswyl seemed something between impressed by this extraordinary courtesy and suspicious; since the latter was his usual mode, Pen gave more weight to the former. The long summer twilight had faded into full dark; the porter lent them a lantern, to be returned on the morrow, which Thala dutifully took charge of.

As they were making their way back through the shadowed streets of Kingstown, Oswyl said, "That went more easily than most of my encounters with kin lords. I should keep you around, Penric."

"Mm, I don't think it was all my doing. Wegae seems a man who'd rather be back in his university life, except without the poverty. No one misses the poverty. And he probably wouldn't be willing to give up his marriage for it, either."

"Understandable."

They were climbing the Templetown stairs when Penric, noting the private moment, thought to ask, "Whatever happened to Inglis's heartthrob, Tolla kin Boarford? His letters stopped mentioning her, and he's not said anything to me since I've been here."

Thala gave a slight twitch, as though she wanted to bring out her notebook, but continued climbing ahead of Oswyl, lantern lifted and eyes resolutely forward.

Oswyl's lips twisted, half grimace, half amused. "She became betrothed to someone else. He's been glum ever since."

Pen reflected on this. "How can you tell the difference?"

Oswyl barked a short laugh. "Glummer, then. I was relieved for him, myself. I did not see how that arrangement could ever prosper, in the long run, after what happened to her poor brother. I thought he should rest content with her forgiveness, which he did surely earn, and not bay for the moon."

"Did you say so?"

"Of course not."

Penric grinned, and saved the rest of his breath for the climb.

Reaching the Templetown heights, they stopped first by what proved to be a sort of boarding house for single female devotees of the Father's Order, where Oswyl scrupulously saw his assistant safely inside. They parted company then, heading toward their respective beds.

Pen was entirely ready for his. He wondered if he might attend on the princess-archdivine in his day dirt and wash after, to speed things up. He didn't want to risk knocking at her chambers after she'd retired. And it wasn't as though he had any definitive news to report, just a mess of miscellaneous information and far too many foxes.

Des commandeered his mouth to speak aloud, breaking through his bleary musings. "Pen."

"What?"

"Ask Learned Hamo what sorceress held Magal's demon before her."

Pen stopped short in the street, his tilting mind seeming to whirl onto a whole new axis. After a blinking moment, he said, "Huh."

"Because there were two victims in that clearing, and Oswyl is only asking after the history of one of them."

"A man would have to be mad..."

"Some men are."

"This is a great leap, Des. With not nearly enough evidence to hold it in the air. Oswyl would sniff at my fancies."

"So good you are a member of the white god's order and not the gray's, then. Are not furious fancies in His gift?"

"Along with obscene verse, but yes."

"*Ask*, Pen," she repeated, a little impatiently. "We just need an answer, not an argument."

"Aye." He changed directions and began striding toward the Bastard's chapterhouse, recalculating people's bedtimes and willingness to be visited at them by a grubby, overexcited sorcerer. Within a few paces, he was jogging. He wasn't actually sure if Hamo lived in at the chapterhouse, the way Magal had. Well, the porter would know his address if not. If anyone else besides Pen and Oswyl was likely to be haunting the night over this matter, it was Hamo.

He arrived breathless to be scrutinized by the night porter, whom they'd briefly interviewed yesterday, and who thus recognized and admitted him even without his whites and his braids. The man tried to make Pen wait in the stone-paved hall while he went to inquire if Hamo would receive him, but Pen dogged his heels, and he hadn't quite the nerve to insist. Their first stop was Hamo's work chamber. Pen was not too surprised to see yellow candlelight sifting through the doorway.

Hamo squinted up from his writing desk, his quill paused in air. He was still dressed in his most formal white tunic from the funeral, although his outer robe and braids hung on a peg on the wall. "Ah. Learned Penric. What brings you to me at this—"

Pen blurted, "The sorceress who held Learned Magal's demon before her. Was it a Learned Sverda?"

Hamo's gray brows rose in surprise. "Svedra, but yes. Why do you ask?"

Pen let his shoulders thump against the door-frame. The name felt like a stone thrown into a murky pond, creating agitation but no clarity. "Mention of her came up earlier this evening, in connection with an investigation she once performed as a Temple sensitive."

"She performed many such, in her time," said Hamo. "Why don't you come sit down? You look a little, ah..." He did not complete the description, but Pen didn't doubt it. Hamo waved the anxious, and curious, porter back to his post. Deprived of his chance to eavesdrop, the man seemed to depart in some disappointment.

Pen pulled a chair around and sank into it. And then felt at a loss, his thoughts all so newly disarrayed.

"What brought up Svedra?" Hamo prompted him, setting aside his quill and papers.

"I hardly like to say yet. It's all wild supposition."

Hamo's eyes narrowed. "Go on anyway."

"What if—" Penric paused, Oswyl's remarks about not leading a witness dancing in his head. "Do you remember any of her assignments as *particularly* fraught?"

Hamo leaned back in his chair and tapped his fingers against each other. "Not especially, but I don't know them all. I'd only been her supervisor for five years before she had her fatal stroke a few months ago. She'd held her demon for over three decades. I may have been her appointed Temple bailiff, but she was much my elder in age and experience. She mostly chose her own tasks and went where she pleased. Which tends to be the way of senior sorcerers. Sorceresses even more so." He winced in some memory he did not confide.

This wasn't getting there—fast enough—Pen led anyway. "About three years ago, she was called out to lend her Sight and expertise to a domestic murder inquiry involving Baron Halber kin Pikepool, yes?"

Hamo's attention sharpened. "An unpleasant fellow, by her remarks. Yes, she was in and out on that several times. Trips to the country, and much back and forthing to the Father's Order, the city magistrates, and the Hallow King's court. There were disputes over jurisdictions, which we tried our best to leave to them. The gods having no such boundaries." He hesitated. "But I thought the man was dead. All disposals in the hands of higher Powers now."

"There was a letter. But not a body, nor any eyewitness account of one."

"Mm...?"

"Imagine..." When out on thin ice, move fast, had been a lesson of Pen's canton mountain boyhood. Did it apply here? "Picture a proud, hard man who has lost everything, and been brought as low as humanly possible, facing an ignoble death. Who did it to himself, but only blamed others." *Indeed, there's only half a chance his wife was the infertile one*, Des put in. "Fled from justice into self-exile, but then, for whatever reason…" Yes, why? Pen was having a hard time positing why a fellow who had got away clear would put himself back at such risk. *That's because you don't think like that,* said Des. *Thankfully.* "This is all utter speculation, you understand."

"Go *on,* Learned Penric," said Hamo, more tightly.

"Suppose he came back for revenge on those he blamed and hated for his downfall. And found the sorceress whose accusation had destroyed him beyond his reach, but her Temple demon…not." Pen took a gulp of air. "Maybe Magal was no one to him, just a barrier he had to get through to reach his real target."

Hamo gripped the table edge, bent his face down, and swore. Short, horrible, heartfelt words.

Ah. Maybe telling Hamo all this so soon had not been such a good idea. Although witnessing Magal's body had been dismaying, Pen had to admit there had been an element of stimulating intellectual puzzle to it all. For Hamo, this had to be a much more personal outrage.

The more so, Des pointed out, *as Hamo himself put Magal in this harm's way, by choosing her to receive Svedra's demon.*

Ouch, thought Pen weakly. He swallowed, feeling a bit sick.

When Hamo raised his face, it was gray with new tension. "That is a grotesque idea."

"Truly. But it may explain why a woman whom no one disliked..."

"Yes." Hamo drew a long breath, letting it out slowly. He lowered his hands from the table edge to his lap, where he clenched them, perhaps to conceal their shaking. After a moment, he said, "Do you really imagine Baron Halber kin Pikepool is still alive? Why?"

"Well... One hears of such things. There was such a case in Greenwell Town, when I was a boy. A man came back from the wars after his wife had remarried. It was something of a mess. Or men reported lost at sea, who turn up years later."

"And how many cases where no one came back, making nothing to remark? No tale worth repeating? One hundred to one? Five hundred to one? The exception always gets more attention than the rule. I'm not sure you should race off down this road too quickly."

"I'm not sure I should, either," Pen said frankly. "But I don't think I would have evolved the notion at all without Halber's tale to start the trail of thought." Des sent him an impression of a throat-clearing noise, and he corrected, "We would have," which only caused Hamo to squint at him.

"What does Locator Oswyl think of your theory?"

"I haven't tried it on him yet. I can't imagine it will please him. He prefers firmer evidences."

"I thought you were seeking such, today?"

"Oh." Getting practiced, Pen made short work of describing his and Inglis's day in the woods, the encounter with Treuch, and the elusive scattering of the kin Pikepool foxes. It did not make Hamo look any happier.

"As a suspect, or at least a man engaged in suspicious activities, this forester Treuch does have the advantage of being certainly alive, and present in the area," Hamo pointed out.

"There is that. Baron Wegae didn't seem to see him as a, a plotting sort of fellow, but who knows? Maybe..." Pen hesitated. "Would you be able to look back over any records the chapterhouse may maintain of Learned Svedra's assignments, and see if there is anything, mm, overlooked? Other possibilities?"

Hamo grimaced. "Tomorrow. In full light, yes. I will."

"Tomorrow," Pen went on, "we're all going up again to look around the old kin Pikepool manor and forest. If the demon is indeed in a fox, and we find it, maybe...it will tell us some more." *How*, Pen couldn't guess.

"If you do find this fox—or Magal's demon howsoever contained—bring it to me unharmed."

"I'll try, sir." Pen hesitated. "What will you do with it?"

Hamo pressed the heels of his hands hard over his eyes, which emerged blinking and reddened. "I have no idea. Yet." He added under his breath, "And here I thought I was finally going to *sleep* tonight..."

Penric stretched in his chair, the day's aches catching up with him, his penalty for sitting down. As Hamo did not at once add more, he rose. "I should go. We mean to start out early."

Hamo nodded, waving a weary dismissal. "Yes. Thank you."

"If we find anything more definite, I'll try to let you know as soon as I can."

"Please."

"And if you find anything...I'll stop back in tomorrow night after we return?"

"Do, yes."

As Penric reached the door, Hamo spoke again. "Penric..."

"Sir?"

"If this mad murderer, whosever he may prove to be, is still seeking our demon-fox, and you are seeking this same fox... Well, just be careful up in those woods, yes?"

"Ah." *There's a thought I should have had sooner.* "Quite so, Learned." Pen touched his thumb to his lips in a parting salute, and took his leave.

PENRIC, OSWYL, and Thala rendezvoused with Baron Wegae, trailed by his porter-and-groom Jons, in the street before his townhouse while the morning air was still dew-damp. They rode through Kingstown in sleepy silence to the north gate, and out it to the main installation of the Royal Society of Shamans. This had once been a farm beyond the city walls, but the town had grown up around it since, the original wattle-and-daub buildings shouldered aside by more substantial structures. The old rustic fences along the street were replaced by an imposing wooden palisade, shielding the Society's secrets.

They threaded through it all to the menagerie yard, formerly extensive royal stables. Penric had visited here a few days ago at Inglis's invitation to witness the sacrifice of an elderly and tame lynx spirit into a half-grown lynx cub, on its way to making a great beast rather more desirable than a worm. The young shaman performing the ritual cuts under the close supervision of his elders had been visibly nervous, but the animal had been strangely serene, and Penric had been put in mind of those tales of people on their deathbeds going gladly to their gods. Except messier, Pen supposed.

No bloody rituals going on this morning, but the last of the short night's cobwebs blew off Penric's brain as he took in the unexpected group that awaited them. Not just Inglis, but three more, yes, shamans were sitting together on the mounting blocks, holding their horses' reins and chatting. All dressed for a day in the country like Pen's party—riding trousers and sturdy boots, with light shirts or sleeveless tunics in anticipation of the day's heat.

Inglis looked up, waved, and rose to make introductions.

"These are my friends Nath"—a big burly fellow, perhaps Oswyl's age—"Kreil"—the bouncy-looking young man in question gave a cheery salute—"and Lunet." The last was a young woman with sandy-red hair and a smattering of freckles across her sharp cheekbones. "They've volunteered to help you hunt for your haunted fox, Penric."

Penric grinned in surprise, instantly envious of the shamanic skills of collaboration, although working alone suited him well for the most part. "Ah, so this is what you went off to find last night. Outstanding idea. Thank you!" Pen took over the task of introducing the Grayjays and Wegae. The shamans, royal pets as they were, seemed not in the least daunted by Wegae's rank, and Wegae in turn appeared openly fascinated by them. He wasn't the only one, although Thala stared more covertly. Lunet eyed her with like interest.

They all mounted up and took the road toward the hills, a substantial cavalcade of nine. A lone murderer, however dangerous, must surely be intimidated by these numbers? Penric hoped so. Readily overcome by his curiosity, Pen turned in his saddle and thought, *Des, Sight.*

Inglis's wolf was its usual more-than-wolfish self. The burly, dark-haired Nath certainly bore a bear, deceptively placid within him. If the eager Kreil didn't house a Great Dog, enthusiastic for this outing, Pen would very surprised. Of them all, only the ruddy Lunet lifted her chin and glanced keenly back at him, poised in stillness, instantly conscious of his more-than-gaze. Great Fox, indeed. That might prove handy.

Penric wondered if their Beasts had been matched to their persons in advance, or if the young shamans had taken on aspects of their possessions after acquiring them. Aspirants worked in the menagerie for some time before being paired with their powers, Inglis had mentioned, so perhaps it was more a matter of the two compatible spirits finding each other. Like a person and their god.

Or their demon, Des put in, slyly.

So what does that reveal about me?

You possess the Bastard's own luck?

Eee. And then wondered how literally true that might be.

Lunet looked as if she might be wondering, too.

Thala rode for a while next to Lunet, the two women quietly talking. At a turn onto a wider road, Thala said, "Well, we have one of each right here. Let's ask," and pushed her horse up between Penric and Inglis. Inglis, after a glance back over his shoulder at his foxy colleague, returned the young Grayjay's look of inquiry.

"I am curious," she said to the air between them, like a woman fairly dividing a cake. "Which came first, sorcerers or shamans?"

"It had to be sorcerers," said Penric.

Inglis's mouth took a noncommittal twist.

Lunet called up, "How can you say? The tradition of shamans in the old forest tribes goes back centuries, maybe millennia, and is lost in the fog of time. The traditions of sorcery can hardly go back farther."

"Do a few thousand years seem like a long time to you?" asked Penric. "I think that must be an eyeblink, in god-sight."

"Then no one can really say either one?" prodded Thala.

"I don't get to it by any historical record, missing or not. I get to it by logic," said Penric.

Oswyl had taken over Thala's stirrup-place beside Lunet: the shamaness looked the senior locator up and down with fresh interest. Amusement tinging his voice, he said, "Logic, Learned? I thought that was my Order's task."

"Task it might be, but not sole dominion. Think about it. Shamans may create other shamans, through the slow building of Great Beasts, but who created the first shaman? Or the first spirit warrior, for that matter, since the simpler creation likely came before, and the more complicated later, probably through some trial and error." Penric reflected on this. Wait, maybe not? There seemed an uncomfortable circularity involved. "The period of error must have been a frustrating time, for those involved. Anyway, the gods, and the gifts of the gods, surely came before people." He hesitated in uncertainty at that last sentence. But this was not the place for the deeper debate on the origins of the gods, in all its subtleties. And heat. He forged on, "Since sorcerers are created by the gift, of sorts, of a demon from the Bastard, those powers must have come first."

"The oldest forest stories would have it that the first shaman was a blessing of the Son of Autumn," said Inglis. "No sorcerer required. Those shamanic practices that sorcerers can replicate, and I'll grant you a few—"

You'd better, thought Pen, recalling his Great Earthworm with, well, not pride exactly, but certainly provisional satisfaction.

"—could as well have been learned the other way around." *As you did*, his eye-glint implied.

"And the Bastard, it is said, was the last of the gods," put in Oswyl, though Penric didn't see how he had a stake in the debate.

Thala frowned. "It's all starting to sound like hearsay evidence to me," she said, eliciting a muffled choke of, possibly, laughter from Oswyl. She did not turn in her saddle to check.

"Welcome to the study of history," said Penric genially.

"And theology?"

A sudden silence fell from all three men.

"Maybe...not so much," said Penric at length. Although that was not a conviction based on his seminary studies for a divine. *Nor hearsay.* "But there is no question people can get theology wrong, too."

"People can get almost anything wrong," sighed Oswyl. "Theology cannot be an exception."

"Mm," Penric conceded.

At the next turn, the road narrowed, and the riders strung out and resorted themselves. The early summer sun was making its slow climb into a blue sky, but their shadows still stretched long across the nearby fields, the strokes of the horses' legs sweeping like scissors. From passing farmsteads, cows released from their morning milkings made their clanking way into pastures, and distant voices echoed around the byres and coops and granaries.

Penric took the opportunity to drop back beside Oswyl, displacing Lunet, though not out of earshot, and detailed to him his new theory from last night's inspiration. Well, from Des. He wasn't sure if naming his source would lend weight to his words or not. As Pen had guessed, his argument about the alternate victim elicited more scowls than smiles from the senior locator.

"What did Learned Hamo think of this...idea?" asked Oswyl. That last word seemed deliberately neutral, replacing something tarter, but at least he seemed to be turning Pen's words over in his mind rather than spitting them back outright.

"He didn't think it was impossible. I mean, from the point of view of the sorceress—either one—or their demon. The actual identity of the murderer being another matter."

Oswyl mulled as their horses plodded up the steepening road. "It seems almost a distinction without a difference, from where I stand. Magal's murder is the crime that will go to court. Her killer must still be secured. Everything must still be proved."

"It might cut down your list of suspects. Or at least redirect it."

"Oh? It seems to me it just lengthens it." After a little silence, he added, "I'm not sure it even is a crime to injure or kill a demon. I mean, doesn't your Order dispose of them routinely?"

"Technically, they are given back into the hands of the white god, whence they came. The god disposes." *Or sometimes not*, Pen was reminded. Des's displeased silence at this turn in the conversation was palpable. "It is no more nor less routine than when the machineries of justice hang a criminal. Whose soul must also go on to the gods, or be sundered as the case may be. A consequence not controlled by any executioner, else justice would be sacrilege."

It was Oswyl's turn to say, "Mm," although with less concession in it.

After a longer silence, Penric asked, "Oswyl... have you ever been only part-way through one of your inquiries and been *sure* you were right?"

"Eh? Certainly."

"You'd push for it, yes?"

"No."

"Why not?"

"Because sometimes, I'm proved wrong. Later."

Pen digested this. "I suppose that's all right."

Oswyl glanced aside at him, looked between his horse's ears, and said, "Not if the accused is hanged first."

Pen opened his mouth, had just the mother-wit not to ask *Has that ever happened to you?* and let his jaw sink closed. As Oswyl's was.

No. He had no envy of Oswyl's calling. He'd be sticking with the white god, thank you.

How fortunate for us all, murmured Des. She might be smirking; might be serious. Or both. Pen rather thought both.

Penric leaned into his stirrups as the road angled up and began to switch back and forth, and the lower edge of the kin Pikepool forest tract closed in around them, casting moist green shadows. He begged Des's Sight again, stretching his senses for foxes, or rather, for one animal that might be much more. The surrounding woods grew glorious, colors seeming brighter, limned with life and movement both swift and subtle, but no foxes as such, though he was briefly distracted by the flash of birds and the musky dusk of a badger. The shamans in the party, too, grew more alert, and he wondered how strangely—or akin— they sensed all this, but no one called an alarm before they finally turned aside into the rutted lane leading to the old kin Pikepool manor house and farm.

Approached from the front, the fortress-like house seemed nearly as brown and blank as when seen from the back. They rode around it to the stable yard before encountering any other people.

As they dismounted, an old man emerged from the house, alarm on his features which faded as he spotted Wegae and Jons. "Oh," he said. Pen thought he might have tugged on his forelock if he hadn't been bald. "Young master." His tone was respectful enough, but...ah. *Young master* not *my lord*. Old retainer, then, relict, like the rest of this place, of the prior baron.

"Ah, Losno, good," said Wegae, turning with an air of familiarity. "We will be here for the day. We'll rest the horses in the pasture."

"I'll fetch the lad." The man trudged off to roust out a stable boy, or gardener's assistant, or general young village laborer—it looked as if the one gangling youth held all such posts. He and Jons and the shamans coordinated in setting the tack in a line atop the fence and loosing the beasts. The pasture's current equine occupants looked as dubious about this alien influx as Losno and his lad, although neither of the human hosts bit, squealed, or kicked.

"Losno is the gardener and caretaker," Wegae explained to Penric and the Grayjays, "along with his wife, who sees to the house. As much as it gets, these days. I'll collect them all for you in a moment."

"Please," said Oswyl.

Pen was dismayed to spot five new fox skins tacked to the stable wall, reeking in the sun. A quick check of the stall found it empty, or emptied. Inglis and Lunet joined his examination.

"Can you tell anything by looking at them?" Pen asked anxiously.

"Not...especially," said Inglis. "They all seem alike, if that helps any."

If anyone had killed the wanted fox already, they would likely have been jumped-to by its demon, Pen reflected uneasily. Creating a whole new problem, but clearly it had not happened to the old gardener or his lad. Nor, when they came out in a few minutes, his wife or her scullion-girl, who could have been sister to the boy. Or maybe cousin, or both, rural villages being what they were.

Oswyl sat them all down on a bench beside the back door and, reinforced by Wegae's weedy authority, began a systematic inquiry. Penric listened, hanging back as anonymously as he was dressed, although he did carry his braids tucked away in his inner vest pocket. The pattern of questions was starting to become familiar. The news about the dead sorceress found in the Pikepool woods induced shock and surprise in the four servants, and some haste to assure everyone listening that they'd seen or heard nothing of it. Pen had no idea if any of them were lying, even with a flash of Sight; all he could sense was agitation, and a certain amount of wriggling gruesome curiosity from the boy, which did not require magic to discern. He wondered if Oswyl could tell any more by experience.

No, no one had seen any strangers about the place in the last few days. Nor in the woods, but you'd have to ask Treuch. Who had gone off there to continue his fox-thinning project. Was this unusual? No, not especially. Wouldn't winter be better for pelts? Well, yes. Did Treuch live in the main house, too? Oh, no, not the forester; he had his own little cottage, pointed out a double-hundred paces away at the edge of the woods. It looked more like a hut to Pen, but no shabbier than the other old wattle-and-daub structures scattered about the grounds. No, Treuch had no wife nor children, never had. No skill at courting, when he was younger, though he would have it that the girls were too picky and proud; the housekeeper sniffed. Oswyl, rather than cutting off this discursion, led them on to gossip about the absent man for a bit, but what he made of it Pen could not guess.

They grew, oddly, less gossipy when asked about the three-year-old tragedy of the slain baroness. The two youths had not worked here then, but the old couple had, and had apparently suffered their fill of interrogation about the crime at the time. In any case, they added nothing new or startling to the tale already told. Though the housekeeper sounded grateful to the Temple sensitives who had removed the ghost from the premises, as if it had been an infestation of some especially appalling vermin. Wegae's mouth twisted— remembering his aunt as a person, perhaps.

They were all squirming when Oswyl finally released them back to their labors. The housekeeper did not look too pleased when he assigned Thala to look about inside the manse, taking the grounds for himself. Penric returned to the stable yard where Inglis had been organizing his squad of shamans for a search of the woods.

"Are you sure you should split up like this?" Pen asked dubiously upon hearing the plan.

"We'll be able to cover more ground, faster," rumbled Nath.

"I was thinking of the dangers of perhaps surprising a desperate murderer," Pen said. "He could still be about." Something, certainly, had to account for Treuch's out-of-season fox-obsession. Or someone? Oswyl himself had not yet closed off the notion of more than one man—person—being involved.

"Penric," said Inglis patiently, "we're *shamans*. Would you consider yourself in danger?"

"Er...not forewarned, I suppose. But I have certain physical powers that you all do not possess."

"And we have certain mental ones that you don't."

Penric increasingly wanted to do something about that lack before this trip was done, if he could. But that would require some canny negotiating with the princess-archdivine, and was not the meal upon his plate this day. "Well...be careful, anyway. If you run across any strange men in the woods, don't approach them. Come back for reinforcements first, eh?"

There was a general, unreassuring *meh* in response to this.

"Oh. And if you encounter the forester Treuch, send him back here. Tell him the baron wants to talk to him, but don't mention the Grayjays yet."

It was decided to begin with the sections to the north and west of the house first, in the general direction of the village of Weir, and all meet back here in about three hours to eat and plan the next cast. Unless someone found the demon, in which case they were to inform Penric in the most expedient way they could. They all fanned out and plunged into the tangled green shade.

TWO HOURS of blundering back and forth through his assigned sector brought Pen no prizes, although he did find and spring an iron leg-hold trap baited with pork fat, and two snares. Might the demon-ridden fox have a more-than-natural wariness of such hazards? Pen hoped so.

Casting around the woods with his Sight fully extended was a strange experience in its own right. He could have used it when hunting as a youth, except...

it was so overwhelming. It wasn't like ghosting along with his bow trying to pick out one tasty target, disregarding all the rest; rather the reverse. The whole tapestry of the forest's life folded in upon him, its intricacy interlocking in finer and finer stitching, so that the mere perception, after a time, grew exhausting. His range was short, half-a-hundred paces, or this god-sight would be entirely too god-like. What kind of Mind was it that could hold the whole world like this, all at once, all the time? Could the gods ever close their Eyes and rest from it, even for a short while? And what would happen if They did?

Also, if he were ever the-gods-forbid by some accident blinded, could this substitute for his lost eyesight? He was in no hurry to find out.

Aside from that, Des grew replete ingesting the life from more biting insects than Pen thought possible, and bored enough to attempt exploding a scampering shrew, a pastime he caught up with just too late. He stared down with some disgust at the splatter across his boot. "Really, Des. Are you a two-hundred-year-old woman—"

"Women," she corrected, blandly.

"—or an idle village lad? Even *I* never pulled the wings off flies."

"Somehow, I am not surprised, dear Pen."

And he was reminded, again, that beneath the two centuries' accumulation of human experience and knowledge that she shared so generously with him, she *was* a chaos demon. Which made him wonder, again, what must be going on right now with the *other* chaos demon, thrown so violently backward into worse disorder.

Hot, sweaty, and hungry, he turned his steps back toward the kin Pikepool manor. His pace quickened as he found yesterday's path. Perhaps one of the others had come upon something. Perhaps they were impatiently waiting for him.

He found Oswyl and Thala sitting on the bench by the back door, though with no sign of impatience. Inglis and Kreil lounged cross-legged at their feet, sharing around a pitcher of well water and some of the food they'd brought along. Inglis looked glum and Oswyl grim, but since both were their natural expressions, it didn't tell Pen much.

They all looked up as he trod near. "Ah," said Oswyl. "Find anything interesting, Learned?"

Pen sighed and joined the pair on the ground, grateful to be handed down a cup. "Not so far. How about yourselves?"

Inglis and Kreil both shook their heads, but Oswyl confided, "Treuch's hut shows signs of hosting a visitor. There was a bedroll, and maybe a few too many cups and plates scattered about."

Thala put in, "The housekeeper notes he's had a hearty appetite of late. Since he brings in game for the table to keep the other servants in meat, she can't exactly complain, she said. While complaining." Her lips twitched back in a brief rare smile—she seemed to be sopping up the sober demeanor, as well as the tips on their trade, from her mentor. "Since he keeps to himself by habit, and is not of a cheerful disposition to start with, no changes there."

"Huh," said Pen. "He's not come in yet?"

"Not so far," echoed Kreil.

One could not accuse Treuch of lying about seeing strangers lately, since he hadn't yet been asked. It wasn't odd for a man to have a visitor. It was odd to keep his visitor a secret, however. "It couldn't have been a woman, in the hut?"

"No signs of such in the clothing or clutter, no," said Oswyl.

"That's very interesting."

"I'd be willing to call it so," Oswyl conceded. Which, from Oswyl, was something like a large signal flag. Not that he'd admit to such a thing. But Pen bet he'd be keeping an eye on Treuch's hut.

"Where's Wegae gone off to?"

"Looking over household accounts, and inspecting the place," said Thala. "He seemed to think it was expected of him. I'm not sure his servants appreciate his conscientiousness." Inglis snickered, and tore into his bread and cheese. Penric put down his emptied cup and waved a hand, and Thala portioned him out a share.

Oswyl came alert first, Pen following his gaze to find Lunet jogging back to them. Her eyes were merry, her cheeks flushed beneath their smattering of freckles. Pen's breath caught in anticipation.

She fetched up before them and bounced on her toes, all smugness. "Found your fox," she announced. Even Oswyl was surprised into a smile.

"Ah!" Pen nearly sprang to his aching feet; his spine straightened. "Then it *was* a fox, we were right! Where?"

Thala handed over a cup of water, which Lunet drained, smacking her lips. "Thanks, needed that. The den's nearly in the center of this tract, about as deep into the woods as you can go without starting out again. On a steep slope, really tangled. But there's a hitch. It looks like your demon has gone into a vixen with cubs."

Pen was taken aback. Somehow, in all his imaginings, he'd pictured a dog-fox, a bachelor ready to travel, although upon reflection that had only ever been half the chance.

"She seemed very distressed," said Lunet. "It was hard to tell if that was the demon part, the vixen part, or both. I haven't tried to get too close to her yet. I thought maybe I'd better come get you, first."

"Did she see you? Or sense you?"

Lunet nodded. "She gave me rather a frantic look, before she shook the cubs off her teats and sped away to hunt. Not the usual time of day for a fox to hunt, but I can see why she had to. Six babies. Oh, Mother and Brother, they were so *darling*. All fluff and flurry, tumbling over each other and chewing on their siblings' ears and tails. She barked at them, such a strange sound foxes make, you know, and they retreated inside. I left a brace of rabbits just in front of the den as a peace offering, then I hurried to get you."

Pen wondered what shortcuts a shaman might undertake to hunt—barehanded!—and if they were anything like the easy devastation he could now wreak, if he chose.

"We should get back soon," Lunet went on. "She might become afraid and move them."

Pen pondered this unexpected development. If he'd had trouble imagining the damaged demon's state of mind before, the puzzle was redoubled. The vixen certainly had her own present obsession, and the demon had been imprinted by at least one sorceress who'd been a mother herself. How were the two fighting it out in the animal's brain? Or had they achieved some bizarre sort of cooperation? Women did that…

Sometimes, agreed Des, seeming as fascinated as he was. And he was reminded that of her twelve previous riders, six had once borne children themselves, if all before they'd joined with the demon. Of Des's two centuries of memories, experiences, and disturbing dream-fragments that Pen did not talk about to *anyone,* those intimacies led the list.

Eight, murmured Des, *counting the lioness and the mare.*

Ah. Yes. Quite. So, maybe one of them had been through something like this before. *Des, help me out, here.*

A rather long pause. Then, slowly, as if feeling her way forward herself, Des offered, *Perhaps we'd better ask the vixen.*

"Huh," said Pen aloud, and then as much to his human companions as to Des, "We can't leave her unguarded, out there. Not with all this unexplained fox-slaughter going on."

There was a general murmur of agreement, and a speeding of the consumption of lunch.

As Pen was chewing down his bread and cheese, Nath lumbered across the yard, the last of their hunting party to report in. He looked his companions over. "Treuch not back yet?" he inquired.

"Did you find him?" asked Oswyl, sitting up.

"I met him in the woods, setting snares. He asked who I was. I said I was a visitor come with his lord, who wanted him to come back to the house. He said he would, as soon as he was done with his task. I drew off and waited till he'd gone, then tripped the snare and followed."

"Then he should have come in ahead of you," said Oswyl.

"Did he seem suspicious of you?" asked Inglis. "Accuse you of poaching or anything?"

"No, our exchange was brief. Civil enough, I suppose. Then he limped off."

"...Limped?" said Penric. "He didn't have a limp yesterday. Was it a new injury, could you tell?"

Nath waved a thick hand. "Old, I'd say. He walked with a staff. Big fellow, grizzled beard. Well-spoken, though, for the little he said."

Inglis and Penric looked at each other and blinked. "How old was the man?" asked Penric.

"Maybe the near side of fifty?"

"Not...around forty, dark-haired, lean, about Inglis's height?" asked Pen.

"No, closer to my size. And shape." Nath shrugged bearish shoulders.

"That wasn't Treuch," said Inglis. "Or...it wasn't the man who said he was Treuch yesterday."

"He answered to Treuch, when I called out to him," said Nath.

"What *exactly* did you say to him?" asked Oswyl.

"I said, *Hello there, are you Baron kin Pikepool's forester, Treuch?* and he said...well, he actually said, *What's it to you?*"

"Could be Treuch's mystery visitor," said Oswyl.

"Or just some random poacher," said Kreil, though his ears had pricked with interest.

Really, murmured Des, *young Kreil makes me want to throw a stick, just to see what would happen.* Pen ignored that one. Nath's description made him deeply uneasy, but there were, inevitably, any number of benign explanations for the man, as Pen was sure someone senior to himself would point out.

"What was he using to bait his snare?" asked Inglis.

"A very dead fish."

"Not after rabbits, then," said Pen. "Or anything else you'd want to eat."

"I wouldn't say so, no," agreed Nath.

Oswyl drummed his fingers on the bench, but, being Oswyl, added no more.

It was decided Kreil would stay at the manor with the Grayjays, in case Treuch or the mystery man returned, to help or run messages as needed. Once they'd secured the demon-fox, Pen wanted to secure the bearded stranger as well, if only to settle his doubts, assuming he could persuade the tired, hot shamans to search the woods a second time. That odd exchange with Nath *could* have just been a poacher being cleverly evasive. Or, if he'd been an honest man, he might turn up on his own, in which case Oswyl could evaluate him. Oswyl, Pen was sure, would jump to no conclusions.

Pen, Inglis, and Nath followed Lunet into the forest once more.

THEY'D TRAMPED a good three miles off the path, including laboring in and out of one wrong ravine, before Lunet put a finger to her lips and slowed, her steps becoming stealthy. Pen tracked her pointing hand to a pile of deadfall and wild grapevines on the gully's opposite slope, and unfolded his Sight. The fox family was at home, judging by the warm pile of squirming life he could sense below the thin green screen.

And so was their mother, by the unmistakable density and roil of a chaos demon therein. The roil instantly grew tense and dismayed; for once, Sight ran two ways, instead of Pen's more usual secret spying.

Just as humans were natural enemies of foxes, there was every reason for the demon to presume a Temple sorcerer was an arresting officer come to carry it off to some execution-by-saint, and no savior. That was certainly a grim task both he and Des had carried out before. Des's density tended to daunt lesser demons, and the fact that she was not ascended was apparently no reassurance. Pen did not see how he was to make up for that by any slathering-on of innocent charm to the demon's host this time.

Was this demon ascended? It was the obvious assumption, and yet... *Des, what do you make of her? ...Them.*

Yes, she said slowly, as if herself unsure. *And yet... the burden of care seems reversed. Magal's doing, maybe?*

It took Pen a moment to figure out what Des meant by that. *The demon is trying to look out for the vixen? Like...like a pet?*

Or a child. Which is what people make of their pets, I suppose. She seemed to consider the cubs, and added, *Children.*

"Lunet," Pen whispered. "Let's you and I try to get closer, without alarming the vixen. Don't want her to bolt. You other two stay here, for now."

"She's already alarmed," Lunet whispered back, swiping a strand of rusty hair off her sticky forehead. "She won't bolt till the very last gasp, though. Because of the cubs."

"Right."

Trying to move quietly, Pen and Lunet made their way to the bottom of the ravine and angled up again until they were just a few paces from the den. Lunet wriggled her finger at the ground, and Pen nodded; they both sank down to sit in the leaf litter, he cross-legged, she on her knees. The silence from under the screen of grape leaves matched their own. The gleam of wary eyes, the faint outline of the furry mask, might almost have seemed a trick of the light and shadows in Pen's sight. But not his Sight.

Can the demon-fox still understand human speech? Pen thought to Des. *You were once a mare. And a lioness. Could you then?*

That was two centuries ago, Pen! In any case, no. Neither one had ever been in a human yet to acquire such skills. Going the other way...is not something I've ever done. Thankfully.

Could the fox's brain even process the complexities of human tongues, to pass along to its demon? Pen, who possessed six languages so far, did not underestimate the task. The sounds, presumably, must pass through unimpaired—foxes had keen hearing—but could a demoted demon retain such comprehension? *No spirit can long exist in the world of matter without a being of matter to support it,* the basic Temple dictum ran. Could the skills of a spirit exist piecemeal? Linger for a time, at least?

There seemed no way to find out but to test it.

Oswyl, Pen had noticed, routinely used Thala to speak with any female interrogatees. Possibly another reason for the canny man to value his assistant, which he obviously did. Perhaps the fox shaman could be such an ambassadress?

"Inglis has this weirding voice," he whispered to her. "I've seen him use it to command dogs. And men, though I should warn you it doesn't work on demons. Can you use such to speak to the vixen? Draw her out?"

Lunet frowned, and whispered back, "The voice is more command than enticement. And dogs already have some grasp of speech. Although there are also songs."

Pen didn't think she meant mere Temple hymns; he needed to find out more about that. *Later.* "I've heard there are stronger spells, geases."

She nodded. "Those only last as long as the shaman pours life into them. Or parasitizes some source of life, most handily the subject himself, but that's a more complex and costly compulsion to set."

"Mm." Compulsion in general only lasted as long as it was enforced. Persuasion could linger more usefully. "Try speaking to her, first. Coaxing gently. Keep the message simple."

"What message?"

Any threat to take the vixen to the Bastard's Order, as Hamo had wished, would terrify the demon. With cause. "Offer to take her—and her cubs—to the Royal Fellowship. You have the wherewithal to keep foxes healthy at your menagerie, yes?"

"Of course." Lunet smiled. "Good notion." She walked forward on her knees closer to the shadowed mouth of the den, and crouched again. **"Hey, lady. We mean you no harm. With all these men hunting, we want to take you to a safer den than these woods. My shamans' den. And your children. Will you trust me?"**

The resonance of the weirding voice, though familiar to Pen by now, still made the hairs stir on his arms. The vixen crept forward into the light, wriggling low to the ground, lips drawn back on her white teeth, ears cycling back and forward. Panting in anxiety. Lunet leaned forward to lay her hand up between the two black front paws, and hummed to no tune Pen recognized, faint and eerie.

Slowly, the vixen lowered her muzzle to touch her nose to Lunet's palm.

Communication of some sort achieved, although with the fox, the demon, or both Pen was not sure. Pen thought back to his own immense confusion upon first acquiring Des. He couldn't very well hand the fox a slim volume on sorcery to read up on her new state, despite all the unnatural awareness that seemed to shine from those copper eyes.

"I suppose," Pen murmured, "we must first get them all back to the manor. And then maybe have Wegae lend us a farm cart to take them to town." Or pannier baskets, or something. If he'd been thinking, they might have brought some such transport aids into these woods. "Six cubs. Can they walk that far? Will they follow?"

Lunet seemed to be making inroads with the vixen, her humming becoming a wordless song, the animal relaxing into her moving hands. She stroked the vixen's head, made play with her tufted ears, ran her slim fingers through the ruddy ruff. Half shamanic persuasion, Pen thought, and half simple, honest delight, persuasive in its own right.

Fascinated, Pen crept forward and extended his own hand, only to have the vixen tilt her head and curl her black-edged lip back on a toothy growl. Lunet shot him a look of annoyance, and Pen subsided, feeling weirdly disappointed at his exclusion from this love-fest. *You just want to pet her, too,* Des snickered. The strange communing continued for a few minutes, then Lunet crawled into the den, to return momentarily followed by the half-dozen sleepy and bewildered cubs, who were indeed, as touted, darling. They blinked shoe-button eyes and made a concerted run on their mother's dugs, but the distracted vixen irritably shoved them away. Almost automatically, Pen took a moment to rid them via Des of their fleas and ticks, which drew a sharp look from the vixen—or her demon—but her sudden tension faded again as it was plain the cubs had taken no harm from him.

So, how much of Magal's demon's powers, or control of its powers, did the fox have? Insect eradication was one of the simplest of destructive magics, the first Des had ever shown him back when he'd so inadvertently acquired her. This did suggest the fox-demon might be less dangerous than he'd feared.

Simple, observed Des, *but requiring fine control.*

Magal should have been able to do it, though. And Svedra.

Oh, certainly. The point is, less-fine control is not necessarily less dangerous.

Hm.

"Let's get them all back to the manor," Pen said. Which would give him a bit of time to think. "And then to the Fellowship." Which would give more. This conundrum was going to need it.

Because, having coaxed the trust of both fox and demon, betraying same, in any of the many ways it might be required by his Temple duty, was growing unappetizing.

At Pen's beckoning, Inglis and Nath left their vantage and approached curiously. Pen explained the new plan, and the whole party rearranged itself for the trek. Lunet took the lead, the vixen at her heels. The cubs followed with about the orderliness one might expect of any other six toddlers, which was to say, none. Inglis and Penric secured the flanks, shooing their little charges back into line, and Nath brought up the rear. For all that he smiled at them, the cubs, after a first wary glance back at him, seemed intimidated by his bearish aura. At least they didn't fall behind.

Hostages, Pen thought unwillingly, eyeing the barging balls of fluff. It seemed he'd taken hostages. It didn't make him feel as clever as it should have.

You're feeling guilty about lying to a fox? Des asked, amused. *Only you, Pen.*

Or, perhaps, to a demon. Or both. It would depend on how events played out.

Ah. Yes. Periodically, I am reminded why I like you. A hint of smug possessiveness.

He had nothing to say to that, though he was vaguely warmed.

The floundering cubs were starting to whine their displeasure at the trek, and Pen's lips twitched as he imagined them nagging, *Aren't we there yet, Mother?* The peculiar procession scrambled out at last to more level ground, heading for the main path. Less than a mile to go to the manor.

The arrow came out of nowhere, too fast for Pen to respond, almost too fast for Des. She was barely able to flip it so that it hit the side of the fox flat-on instead of point-first. The animal yelped and spun. By the time the next arrow was in flight, Des, unasked, had speeded Pen's perceptions to match her own. He splintered the second shaft and sent the iron point tumbling, even as he whirled just like the fox, seeking the source.

From his point of view, when Des deployed this defense, the world around him slowed. Lunet was turning, Inglis raising his hand, Nath lifting his head, all with the languor of a bead dropping through honey. The cubs, at their mother's cry, were either crouching or scattering. Pen's gaze sought frantically through the woods for the bowman—*there*, in the cover of those upended tree roots. Pen had just the presence

of mind to snap the bowstring *before* he started running toward the assassin, so that the third shaft was
not aimed at him, but flew wide as the broken ends
whipped into the bowman's face, drawing blood.

He jumped over a fallen log, feeling the strain
of too much power forced through his legs too fast.
Behind him, Inglis yelled, "Look after the foxes!"
and pelted in his wake.

And then he was upon his target. Dizzied—
he felt as if he'd left his wits blown back along his
track. He grabbed the man by his leather jerkin,
hoisted him to his feet, and slammed him against
the nearest upright tree trunk. The bow clattered
to the ground.

It was Treuch, he realized at last, as Des let the
world fall back to normal speed and his lungs labored
for breath—this unnatural bodily debt did have to
be repaid, oh aye, and no extensions. Treuch did not
cooperate with his sudden arrest; he punched his
clenched hands up through Penric's grip and broke
the hold, shoving Pen back. Pen stumbled and came
around again.

I could snap his tendons as easily as his bowstring,
Des offered. Not quite the theologically forbidden act
of murder by magic, but too close for Pen's comfort,

too irreversible. The reminder abruptly cooled Pen's heated head just as Inglis, thankfully, arrived.

"You two!" wheezed Treuch. He reached for the hunting knife at his belt and whipped it out before him.

Pen turned the blade to rust, bursting off in a spray of orange flecks as Treuch slashed. Inglis bellowed, "**Stop!**" and the hilt, passing a bare inch from Pen's belly, dropped from nerveless fingers. The forester's mouth fell open in astonishment, and then, as his eyes rose to meet Pen's, fear. "What—!"

The three men fell into a stiff triangle, fists clenched, chests heaving. Pen seized the teetering moment to try to shift the encounter from ill-considered actions to words. Where he, at least, would be on safer ground. Because shooting at a fox, as Thala might remark, was not normally a capital crime.

Oh, I'd see you safe regardless of your ground, Des purred. But she settled in disappointment as the chance for more chaos died away.

Pen yanked his triple-looped braids from his inner vest pocket and brandished them at the forester. "I am Learned Penric of Martensbridge, Temple sorcerer," he declared, then drew a breath he wasn't quite sure what next to do with.

If he'd thrust a live adder in the man's face, Treuch couldn't have recoiled more sharply.

"I am detaining you..." In the name of what? Legally, Pen only held higher authority over the demon in this jurisdiction, and that bestowed by Hamo. He skipped over that conundrum and went on, "in suspicion of complicity in a murder."

Treuch pushed away, hovering between fighting and running, although Pen thought the fates of his bow and knife should have taught him better than to try the first again. Inglis growled, **"Surrender."**

The man did not so much surrender as seize up, caught between the conflicting demands of terror and shamanic compulsion. "I didn't shoot her!" he all but squealed.

Pen blinked, going still. "I didn't say who was murdered. Or how."

Treuch froze in a different sort of horror, gaping fish-fashion.

"Oswyl will want this," said Inglis.

"*I* want this," said Pen, his stare at Treuch intensifying. Inglis regarded Pen warily.

They were interrupted by the low growl of a fox. The vixen stalked up to them stiff-legged, the ridge of fur standing up on her spine, ears flattened backward. Her copper eyes were bent on Treuch. For all her vicious air she had not the size to be a lethal-seeming threat, as predators went, but no, it wasn't the *fox* that was the true danger here.

"It seems you are accused," said Inglis dryly. Treuch's terror slumped in a rush sheer bewilderment.

The panic transferred to Pen. He stepped hastily in front of the fox, between her and the forester, and cried, "No, you cannot!"

The animal—no, the demon—crouched away from Des's roiling density, the bolt of damaging chaos gathering to pitch at the man dying away again. *Bastard be praised.* Pen wasn't sure if such a blast of unformed magic could have killed Treuch outright, but he was very sure of the unwanted consequences if it did.

"I don't know yet if I can save you, but I do know I can't if you do this!"

Did either demon or fox understand him? Even if more-than-vulpine comprehension flashed in those copper eyes, that didn't make it *human*.

A bow-shot away, the frightened yips of the cubs being forcibly gathered up distracted the vixen part of this unintended creature. She turned once, turned back, halfway to frenzy from all the conflicting demands.

"We have to get these two separated," gasped Pen to Inglis, gesturing blindly at Treuch who now seemed the least of his troubles. He raised his voice. "Nath! Get over here!"

Nath lumbered across the deadfall, his arms full of protesting fox cubs, and said, "Yes, Learned?"

"You and Inglis take Treuch ahead of us to the manor," Pen said. "Lunet and I will bring the foxes." And the demon, he did not say aloud. Did Treuch have the least notion of how much danger he'd just skirted?

If he'd had his way, that first knife-slash would have disemboweled you, Pen, Des noted dryly. *And then nothing would have saved him.*

And Pen didn't think she meant from the fox-demon. He chose to ignore both this and the belated trembling in his belly. His sweating hand still clenched his Temple braids, he discovered, and he shoved them back into his vest pocket. It was a continuing wonder to him how much less, rather than more, freedom that acquiring a responsible authority gave to one. Not at all how he'd pictured his elders, so seeming-powerful, as a child. As Nath bent to release the cubs, who ran to their distrait mother, Pen also decided it must be a more universal condition than he'd ever imagined.

"You"—Pen turned again to Treuch—"your baron has commanded your immediate attendance, and is awaiting you at the manor." Yes, better not to mention the Grayjays quite yet. If the man did break away from his captors, he'd likely be as hard to find in his woods as a fox.

Treuch jerked, taken aback. "What?" Then, "Oh. Young Master Spectacles."

Pen nodded. "He brought us up for the fox hunt." He met Treuch's surly glare. Indeed, Treuch knew what he'd really been hunting, however poorly the sundered fool understood the ramifications. Pen would be taking this up with him as soon as possible, even if he had to get in line behind Oswyl. He gestured at Inglis and Nath. "Go, quickly!"

The pair of shamans, thankfully, didn't question or argue, but each took one of the forester's arms and marched him off between them. Between Nath's hulking size and both their powers, Pen fancied the arrest would hold till they could deliver Treuch to the Grayjays. Treuch glanced in fear over his shoulder at Penric, clearly unaware that this sorcerer-divine might have just saved his life. Twice. So, was that Pen's good deed for the day, or a regret in prospect?

Pen waved at Lunet, and they both turned to the task, *again*, of calming the vixen and collecting her offspring. Six languages at his fingertips, and this was the hardest communication task he'd ever undertaken. They were making their way onto the beaten path when Lunet muttered something annoyed under her breath, put down her trio of cubs, whipped a handkerchief from her trouser pocket, and clapped it to her nose. Pen was startled to see it soaking with red.

"Are you all right?"

She nodded, moving the cloth off her messy lip to say, "The price of shamanic magic is blood. Did you not know?"

"Mm, yes, but I'm still not clear on the how of it."

She shrugged. "Small magics, small price. Larger magics, larger price. But always the same coin."

Pen thought of the array of gruesome scars on Inglis's forearms, which was why, Pen presumed, he wore long sleeves even in hot weather, and never rolled them up unless among his most intimate friends.

Lunet stopped mopping, frowned at her handkerchief, and folded and pocketed it. She bent and chirped to coax her cubs back; they came readily to her arms, and they started off through the woods once more. She allowed them to reach up and lick her face, which seemed to amuse her vastly. Pen swallowed his *urk*, almost.

"There are less convenient ways to spontaneously bleed, trust me," she tossed aside to him, grinning.

Pen wondered what. Or how many different—

Des, with an air of taking pity on innocence, apprised him: *She's talking about monthlies. I imagine that could make for some confusion, for a shamaness.*

Pen kept his eyes up. He trusted his flush from the heat masked his blush. He was relieved when the nose-drip died away, and Lunet stopped using the cubs for a substitute handkerchief.

I have to learn more about this.

Of course you do, Des echoed Inglis's words of—was it only two days ago? At least her tone was more fond.

AS THEY made their way more quickly along the beaten path, Pen's three cubs were fuzzy weights in his arms, warm and charming, but kept sharply nipping at him. Lunet managed to stay unperforated, which seemed backward, given their respective magics. The vixen still seemed to trust Lunet, and her demon was deeply wary of Des, so by whatever internal truce the two had, the animal's body followed along. Pen calculated how to house them all once they arrived at the manor. Probably a stable stall, again. With the bottom door closed to contain the cubs, and the top open to give the vixen the illusion of freedom. Toss in a couple of rabbits, place a basin of water, and it would with luck hold them till it was time to decamp for Easthome. Would Oswyl arrest Treuch?

I didn't shoot her, Treuch had cried. So who had?

Des, did you sense he was speaking the truth?

A pause. *Not sure. He was distressed, and I was busy.*

Well, it was plain Treuch knew something—far too much—about Magal's death. Pen imagined Oswyl had proven ways of getting such things out of men.

Bet we could find ways break him open if Oswyl can't, Des suggested slyly.

Pen bet they could, too, but Oswyl needed more than just knowledge—he needed a case. Father's Order business, that. "Best wait till we're asked," he replied aloud, which made Lunet cast him a puzzled glance.

The path opened out into the meadow on the back side of the manor house. Everyone appeared to have gone within, or elsewhere. They circled to the stables, and Lunet sang the foxes into a suitable stall. Pen breathed relief when he was finally able to swing the lower door shut on them.

"I think you'd better stay with them till I find out where Treuch was taken," he told her, shaking out his tooth-pricked arms. Would they count as shamanic coin? "To keep them calm. And, if necessary, protect them." Pen stared a bit doubtfully at Lunet's slender form, but...powerful shamaness, he reminded himself. If others underestimated her, so much the better. Or so he had found it in his own case. "And, ah—maybe protect everyone else from the vixen. Keep people away from her, certainly."

Lunet nodded understanding, and Pen made his way around the stable block, heading for the manor house. A movement at the edge of the meadow caught his eye—oh, it was just Wegae. Continuing his diligent inspection of his property, presumably. He followed along behind his elderly gardener-caretaker, Losno, who gestured him in his wake and pointed to, yes, that was Treuch's hut in the distant shaded verge.

They were too far away for Pen to hear what they were saying, but Losno turned back and Wegae went on in. Wait, Treuch couldn't be back home already, could he? Surely he must have been delivered to Oswyl just a short time ago.

Someone's in there, said Des. *Not Treuch, no. Someone new. Someone...angry.*

Pen thought the Grayjays had taken inventory of all the manor's servants already. He hesitated, torn between the two curiosities of Oswyl's interrogation of Treuch and this fresh mystery. He took one step each way.

Something's very wrong in that hut, said Des suddenly, and Pen angled toward it, planning to intercept the gardener and ask what was going on. Losno glanced his way and shuffled faster, looking oddly frightened.

Pen. Run!

He didn't think to ask why till he was already in motion. She didn't volunteer his trick of uncanny speed, so maybe the emergency wasn't lethal?

Yet, she said grimly.

Pen sped up on his own, the meadow grass slapping around his legs like thin green fingers trying to delay him.

Thumps echoed from the hut. He bounded up the porch and yanked open the door on murky dimness. Shapes moved within it. *Des, light!* His vision brightened and he saw a small table toppled over, Wegae lying on the plank floor, his hands flung up across his bleeding face. His spectacles spun aside, just out of his reach. A heavyset older man with a staff in his hand heaved forward, stamping down a booted foot; the glass crunched horribly, and Wegae cried out as though he himself had been struck.

"Eh?" The bearded face of the stranger jerked up at the light from the door and Pen's awkward entry.

Was this the not-Treuch that Nath had encountered in the woods a few hours ago? It seemed they wouldn't have to hunt him down after all. Lucky chance? Pen had barely opened his mouth to demand explanations, or say he knew-not-what, when the man lunged toward him and the staff whipped around at his head. *Ah. Bastard's luck.*

Pen's duck this time was with demonic haste, or he'd have won a fractured skull. But the miss did not impede the attack; the man shifted his thick hands and the staff's other end followed up near-instantly.

If Des had managed to burst it into splinters just before, and not just after, it smacked into Pen's forearm, that would have been quite helpful. As it was, he yowled and jolted back, arm throbbing and just short of broken.

Singlestick fighter. Trained and dangerous. And possibly berserk, because shattering half of his weapon didn't even slow him down. He just reversed it, the sharp, jagged end Pen had inadvertently supplied now turned into a short spear; it jabbed savagely. Battlefield reflexes? Pen squawked and burst the whole thing into blazing sawdust in the man's hands.

That finally got through to him, or at least his eyes widened in astonishment. It still didn't give him pause: he kept on coming, hands widening out through the cloud of smoke and flames, seizing Pen's neck. Which was what Pen was due, he supposed, for so rudely interrupting a murder in progress. Wegae yelped and scrambled to his feet, blindly feeling around for some sort of weapon or shield. Pen hoped he'd find something. Meanwhile, he was on his own.

Not quite, said Des. And reached out to snap the bones inside their assailant's hands. The muffled sound, so close to Pen's ears, was sickening. Fair payment for the spectacles?

The strangling grip weakened; a last attempt to wrench his neck fell away in what Pen hoped was excruciating pain. For someone besides himself. Choking, he fell back, trying desperately to open some distance between himself and this murderous madman. Because even a sorcerer needed a moment to plan his attack, or defense.

Not this fellow, apparently. Every movement he'd made since Pen had broken in upon him had felt mindless. Practiced? Because in the middle of a such a fight, there was hardly time to think. Maybe Pen should have trained like that. But, sunder it, a divine entrusted with a demon was *obligated* to think before he acted. He was sure that was in his Temple oaths somewhere, by implication at least.

"It's Uncle Halber!" Wegae shrieked from the side.

"Figured that out!" Pen wheezed back.

"Quit fighting, you fool!" Wegae shouted. Oh— not at Pen, for he followed up with, "He's a sorcerer!"

Halber had seemingly not quite realized it yet, or else he was beyond reason, but the result was likely not the quelling one Wegae had envisioned. He plunged at Pen with sudden and renewed ferocity, eyes wide and glaring. Pen barely evaded a thunderous kick. Then Halber actually tried to grip his belt knife in his swelling hands. And *succeeded*, Bastard's tears.

Having a few moments longer this time as he was chased around the small room, Pen varied his defense by heating the hilt. *Pen*, Des chided, *this is not the time for showing off.* It had actually started to glow before Halber finally dropped it clattering to the planks. He bellowed in pain.

We have to stop this, Pen thought. *Before I get killed and you end up in Wegae.*

*Mm...*Des hummed.

His demon, Pen decided, wasn't so much brave as *vicious. Are you* playing *with him?* Only his speed allowed him to dodge a few more fierce kicks.

Wegae had finally located an iron frying pan. He managed one good whack—not hard enough—before he was punched aside again. The pan flew away with a clang. That Halber bent over his fists in agony after was small consolation.

Try to get your hand on his lower back, said Des. *Just for an instant. This is going to take some precision.*

Bastard's tears! Well, give me all the speed you can, then.

For the first time, Pen went on the attack, or something vaguely resembling attack. He spun around to face Halber as the man closed the distance trying for another mighty booted kick. *Left, right, under, over?* The world slowed to its utmost, and Pen, tapping his lips with his thumb, crouched to make springs of his legs. He bolted off the floor and into the air, one hand bracing on Halber's shoulder, curling his knees to avoid slamming his feet into the low ceiling beams. He swung his other hand, still tingling from the singlestick blow, down to flatten his palm against the man's lower spine. His touch was quite soft.

The bone-crack this time was sudden, sodden, and final.

Halber's nerveless legs splayed out, and he dropped like a bludgeoned ox. "*Eh?*"

Pen's feet kissed the planks, and his legs bent double to absorb the shock of his landing. He came up and staggered a few steps before finding his balance. His body was dangerously, boilingly hot from the rapid deployment of his magics, even as the pace of the world came back to itself once more. He stood gasping, sweat running down his face, netting in his eyebrows, dripping from his chin. Bending, he tore off his boots and socks, vest and shirt, in a desperate bid to cool.

On the floor, Halber snarled filthy curses and threats and struggled to stand. Futilely, as his body from the waist down had gone as flaccid and helpless as a sack of custard.

Wegae recovered his pan and, holding it like a shield in one hand with the other out before him to feel his way, blundered fearfully to Pen's side. "He said he was going to *kill* me," he choked. "I mean, I always knew he despised me, but I didn't know he hated me that much!"

"—and that bitch your mother—!" Halber picked up his diatribe; his violence, blocked from physical expression, finding its outlet in words. Venting. Spewing. The targets of his obscene wrath seemed to include Wegae, Wegae's mother, Penric— not by name, but Pen presumed that *you bloodless blond Bastard's tit* meant him—all Temple sorcerers, the demonic fox, and Easthome judges. And his baroness and his brother, both of whom were long dead as far as Pen knew.

Penric steered Wegae to the door. "Run to the house. Find Oswyl. Find everyone. Bring aid."

Wegae needed help determining which brown blur in the distance was the manor house, but once Penric gripped his head and got him aimed, he stumbled off in the right direction.

Penric turned back to the hut, trying to figure out what in the gods' names had just happened here. Deposed Baron Halber come back for revenge, obviously, but never before had Pen found the proof of one of his theories to be so appalling.

Deprived of an audience, Halber had fallen silent. Pen could believe he really had fought in a mercenary company, after he'd fled Easthome three years ago. Would Penric's brother Drovo have turned into something this brutal, if he'd survived his camp fever? Pen shuddered.

Halber's broken hands must hurt, for he was curled around them, but Pen supposed he wasn't feeling further pain, or anything else, from his lower body. *Is that right, Helvia?* he asked tentatively. Because the knowledge of exactly what injury to devise and how must have come from her, or Amberein.

More or less. She didn't sound happy. Although not nearly as distraught as Pen. He'd never before inflicted a magical wound so intimate and calculated.

But controlled, put in Des. *Consider that.*

Deep bruises were starting on Pen's forearm and
neck. Any number of pulled muscles were already
rioting in protest. He bent to collect his shirt, shrug-
ging it on. He wasn't ready for the rest yet, but he
did don his Temple braids, pinning them crookedly
to his left shoulder. He had to be the least dignified
divine ever, bloodied and sweat-soaked, blond queue
gone wildly askew, judging from the hair hanging in
his face. He retied it while trying to collect his scattered wits, staring down in bafflement at his abrupt
victim, who stared up in loathing.

Pen cleared his throat. "Do you normally try to
murder people you've just met?" Although that was
what a soldier did, he supposed.

More cursing, if wearier and not so loud.

Pen worried. If the man died later from this
injury that Pen had done him, would it count as
death by demonic magic? Could he still lose Des to
the Bastard's peculiar justice, which had nothing to
do with the vagaries of any human court?

Had Des, if not outright sacrificed herself for
him, certainly risked such a fate?

I wouldn't fret, she said coolly. *He's bound to be
hanged first.*

A dubious hope.

Pen was sure he needed Oswyl here, with Thala and her notebook, before he started interrogating suspects, but he had to know. "*Did* you shoot Learned Magal in the woods three days ago?"

Halber glowered at him from his thatch of hair and hatred. "That stupid Temple woman? It was the only way to get that hag Svedra's demon out of her to destroy it. If it hadn't jumped to that accursed fox, I would have been half done."

"Half...?"

"And then there was that bitch my brother's wife. And her whelp Wegae. It was all her doing from the start. Trying to take what was mine—for *that* weed."

"Surely...you didn't imagine that if you could murder all those people, you could get everything back? Your rank, your property, your place?"

Halber snorted contempt. "If I can't have it, let no one do. Especially not *them*." He turned his head away, spat, and added, "Didn't have much more time. He's *spawning*."

Pen blinked. "Er...shouldn't it have been a greater concern how you are to present your soul to your god?" Although *Which god?* was a good question. The Father of Justice was right out. The

Mother and the Daughter likewise. The Bastard, god of all leftovers, seemed unlikely after Magal, although there was no telling. The Brother was a god of vast mercy, as Pen had reason to know, but…

"Curse the gods. Curse the world. Curse… everybody."

Comprehensive, murmured Des.

"So…so you went through all this effort, perpetrated all this pointless cruelty, just to make yourself *feel better*?"

A wordless snarl.

Pen's voice went dry; he couldn't help it. "Is it working?"

Halber's arms flailed in helpless rage, but he couldn't reach Pen. He tried to the last, though.

Pen went back out to the porch and sank down on the wooden steps. The late afternoon was still bright and sunny. Perfect picnic weather, or to go fishing. After that abysmal bout of Halber, it felt as though it ought to have been midnight, and raining.

Pen ached. And felt ill. "Well. That was ugly."

"You foresaw it," said Des. Comfort? Cold comfort?

"It's one thing to foresee. Another to see. It turns out."

She was kindly silent.

He looked up to find Oswyl tromping toward them across the meadow, followed by a mob. Thala and her notebook, half-blind Baron Wegae being led by the hand of Jons his servant, Nath and Kreil bracketing Treuch between them. Inglis. Pen was relieved to see Inglis. They'd need a couple of men to get the helpless Halber back to the house.

Oswyl shot Pen a look of sharp inquiry as he neared.

"Your prisoner"—Pen gestured over his shoulder—"is restrained. Have at him."

"Baron kin Pikepool says you saved his life."

"Mm, probably. His lunatic uncle was just warming up to beat him to death, I think."

"You coming in?"

"Rather not. I've had enough for now."

"Hm." Oswyl frowned in concern at him, but led the party inside.

He left the door open, though, and Pen, despite himself, ended up listening shamelessly.

After some noises indicating them getting Halber sitting up, Oswyl began with what were by now familiar preliminaries, with no cooperation from his surly suspect. But Oswyl shortly managed to get Halber and Treuch started in on each other, which perhaps explained why he'd dragged Treuch out here. The exchanges of blame and recrimination were better than any interrogation an inquirer could have devised, with or without red-hot irons. Oswyl only prodded them a little when they started to slow down.

"It wasn't my fault!" Treuch declaimed. "He didn't tell me *why* he needed me to get the Learned up there!"

Halber snorted contempt. Thala's stylus scratched busily.

"He told me to tell her there was a badger I thought was possessed by an elemental. That I needed her to see if it was so, and take it away to her Order."

Certainly a routine task for a Temple sorcerer, if important. A shrewd draw. If Halber had known little of sorcery before his first arrest, he'd likely had an opportunity to learn after.

Which was why Halber had pressed his old lackey Treuch to be his stalking-horse, of course. He'd been afraid Svedra's former demon might have recognized him. Possible, that.

"I didn't even see! He told me to just bring her and leave her. Tell her I was going to check if the creature was still in its den. I didn't see anything!" Treuch somewhat spoiled this impassioned defense by adding, "He should have hidden her right then, not gone fooling off after that fox all by himself. It wasn't my fault!"

"That will be for the judges to decide," Oswyl sighed.

After Thala collected signatures from the listening witnesses, the men collaborated on devising a makeshift litter for Halber to be lugged away to the manor house. He'd be put on a cart to the Easthome magistrates as soon as a horse could be harnessed. Treuch whined horribly at the news that he was to be taken along tied to the rail. Oswyl was plainly unmoved by his protests. By nightfall, they would both be someone else's problem, though Pen was certain the senior locator would have reports to write.

Oswyl came out on the porch as Nath and Jons maneuvered the litter down the stairs and marched away with it. Treuch followed with the dolor of a mourner in a cortege, Thala keeping a close watch on him. Kreil guided Wegae like a loyal dog. Oswyl lingered a moment to stare oddly down at Pen.

"Restrained? His spine is broken. Did you realize?"

"Oh," Pen sighed, "yes."

"How did that happen?"

"In the fight," Pen answered, although that likely wasn't exactly what Oswyl was asking. "Wegae witnessed it, I believe." How much the poor fellow could *see* being an open question.

"Hm, yes, his description was dramatic, if confused. He sounds wildly grateful to you."

"I don't believe he could have succeeded in defending himself from Halber. The man was terrifying."

"And yet you are standing, and Halber is…not."

Not ever again. "I'm sitting," Pen pointed out.

Oswyl puffed something not nearly a laugh. "Baron Wegae is coming with us to lay his deposition and accusation. What about you?"

Pen gestured to Inglis, leaning against the porch post and glummer than ever. "The shamans and I will be taking the foxes to their menagerie, for now. Best to keep them well separated from Halber and Treuch. I'm not sure I could control the fox's demon if she sees them."

"Ah." Oswyl frowned uneasily. "You would know best, I suppose. We'll need a deposition from you, too, in due course."

"I won't be hard to find. I imagine I'll be splitting my attendance between the menagerie and the princess-archdivine, for now. And Hamo. I promised to call on Hamo tonight. I didn't expect to have this much news for him." Pen wondered if he'd need to apologize for sending Hamo on a blind search through his records all day.

"Oh. Yes. I had better speak to him myself. Although the next-of-kin may need to come first. Tell him to look for me tomorrow." Oswyl blew out his breath. "I hope he will be pleased with our success."

"Ah. Hm." Pen wasn't sure if he should speak this thought aloud. "Best you keep Hamo separated from Halber and Treuch, too. For a few days, till he calms down."

Oswyl's brows flicked up. "Really?"

"Hamo's a smart man. I suspect the stupidity of this entire revenge escapade is going to enrage him beyond measure."

"…How far beyond?"

"He's a man with responsible authority." *And a chaos demon.* "Just don't…bait him. Tempt him."

Oswyl took this in, thoughtfully. After a moment, he murmured, "I am advised."

"Thank you."

Tilting his head, Oswyl asked, "And how tempted were you?"

"Less than Hamo would have been, I'm sure. But there were difficult parts."

Oswyl glanced after the retreating litter. "I shall like to hear more about that. When there is time. But Penric…"

"Hm?"

"Subduing a criminal who violently resists always has elements of risk. For everyone. It comes with the task. Things can happen too fast, and no one is in control. It's understood, in my Order."

"Some risks"—Pen scratched absently at the drying scabs on his arms, palpated the throbbing bruise—"are different than others." He looked up. "Are all your cases this awful?"

"No. Well, some." Oswyl's gaze at him was less than reassured. "We'll talk later," he promised, and hurried after his charges.

"So." Pen looked up to Inglis. "We have a lost demon to shepherd."

"Aye."

Sometimes, Inglis's gloomy silences could be quite soothing. They walked together toward the stable.

THE FOX family was loaded into pannier baskets, one pair carried over the haunches of Pen's horse and the second on Lunet's. The young passengers whined for a time, restrained under closed lids, but then settled down to sleep. The vixen was granted the courtesy of being allowed to ride behind Lunet in her own basket with the top fastened open. Pen tried to persuade himself that her cynical expression, as she was trundled along, was merely the usual one for a fox. It was nearly dark by the time they'd transported their furry charges to the menagerie of the Royal Fellowship.

A spare stall was swiftly readied, the animals bedded down for the night with small protest. Pen made promises to the vixen to return on the morrow, with as little assurance that they were understood as that he could keep them. The tired shamans could at last depart to find their own beds, with Pen's repeated thanks.

And Pen could crawl atop his horse one more time—he used the mounting block—and make his way up through Kingstown to Templetown and the chapterhouse of the Bastard's Order, for what he prayed would not be too difficult a report.

THE NIGHT porter, recognizing Penric, let him in without demur despite his bedraggled appearance. Pen found his own way to Hamo's workroom. The candles were burning late as before, although Hamo had put down his quill and sat with his elbows on his writing table, his face resting in his hands. He jerked up at Pen's knock on the door-jamb, blinked reddened eyes, and said in a blurry voice, "Ah. Good. You're back at last." Had he been waiting up?

Pen fetched his own chair and dropped into it.

Hamo looked him over. "Five gods. Were you dragged by a horse?"

"I feel like it," admitted Pen, running his hand over his grimy face. *Yech.* "Not quite. But let's have your tale first."

Hamo pursed his lips but complied, shoving a thin stack of papers across his table to Pen. "I found four accounts from Svedra that looked promising. As she grew older, they tended to become more laconic, which was not as much help as you'd think, since they required more cross-checking. Her most difficult cases from the past five years, that may have left someone angry but not confirmed dead. I can look back farther if needed."

Pen took them up and squinted through them. He puffed relief at finding Halber's case second in the sheaf. "Locator Oswyl will wish to see all of these. If only for his own reassurance. He means to call on you tomorrow." He forced himself to at least look at the other three, but set them down when he realized that Oswyl would be better able to evaluate them, and that he was just stalling. "But he has former baron Halber kin Pikepool in custody, and his confession."

Hamo went stiff in his chair. Pen could feel his demon stirring from where he sat. Dark, with red flashes like heat lightning.

"Halber had been in hiding up at his old forest manor, where we flushed him out. Not being a man who does things by halves, Halber also tried to murder his nephew Wegae. Crime of opportunity, as nearly as I could tell. Caught in the act, fortunately for both Wegae and for Oswyl's case. He also had a try at me. I don't think we need count me. I'm redundant to need."

Hamo's fists curled into tight balls. "Did he shoot Mags?"

"Yes. Had his thrall lure her with some tale of a badger possessed by an elemental. Up to his home woods, where he laid an ambush. His aim was to destroy her demon. Magal was just…in his way. He said."

A little silence, broken by a growl. "Where is he now?"

"I don't actually know," said Pen, glad he could answer, or not-answer, that question honestly. "Wherever the Grayjays usually take dangerous suspects in Easthome." Not that Hamo couldn't find out, but anything to slow him down…

As Hamo's tight-lipped silence thickened with menace, Pen went hastily on, "He's not going anywhere. Can't. His back is broken, and both his hands. If your heart wishes him pain, I promise you he has it. If you wish him dead, well, the magistrates of Easthome will accomplish that task for you as well. Magal's family and friends may not even have to endure his trial, if they decide to execute him for the murder of his wife, for which he's already convicted. The wheels of justice will grind him fine, and soon." Pen hesitated. "No need to…compromise yourself."

Hamo looked up, the peculiar list of injuries perhaps penetrating whatever red haze his mind was lost in. His voice rough, he asked, "Are you com-promised, Penric?"

"Mm..." Pen shrugged. "Possibly a little. Oswyl seemed to think that the fact I injured Halber in the course of his resisting arrest would pass unquestioned. That it was by...more-than-physical means might not, if it were looked into by a hostile inquiry. I've never done anything like this before. Well, there was that time with the kin Martenden brothers, but I only set them on fire—never mind," Pen ran down before his mouth did him more harm than good.

Hamo unclenched his teeth. "Should anyone ask," and now his voice went soft, which was some-how not less alarming, "you may say you acted under my authority, Learned Penric."

"Thank you," said Pen. He was fairly sure the princess-archdivine's cloak would cover him, but more layers wouldn't hurt, and it gave Hamo a straw of usefulness to clutch. *Useful to us, at least,* Des murmured, a trifle sardonically. Time for the next diversion: "And also, with welcome help from some shamans Inglis brought from the Royal Fellowship, we located Magal's lost demon. It was indeed in a fox."

Hamo sat up, his tension thinning like slate-gray clouds shredding in a wind. Des's attention upon her internal counterpart eased. "Oh! You took it alive? Is it here? What condition—"

"It turned out to have lodged in a vixen with six cubs, which had some strange consequences."

"It is ascended, surely."

"Well, yes, but in an odd mode. It seems to be, I'm not sure how to put it, taking *care* of the vixen. And her children."

Hamo sat back, nonplussed, but then after a moment sighed. "That would be Magal, I suspect. It sounds like her. Svedra was a woman more in the style of your Ruchia. Very...forceful."

Pen wondered what less flattering term Hamo had swallowed. Des snickered at him, or possibly at them both.

"I have some ideas of what might be done with her," Pen put forward. "The vixen, that is. Uh, and the demon." Or he would, when he'd had a chance to sleep and recover. Hamo could take this burden of care from him with a word, Pen knew. Half of him was almost weary enough to let him, but... "Yesterday, you said you were thinking on it?"

Hamo scrubbed his hands through his hair, grimacing. "There are only two choices. First, have the Saint of Easthome remove the damaged demon to the god."

Of *course* the Bastard's Order at the royal capital would have its own saint at hand. Although not, probably, at call, from what Pen had experienced of saints. Such directly god-touched men and women did not owe their primary allegiances to the *Temple*, after all. Des flinched.

"Or second," Hamo went on, "sacrifice the fox and transfer whatever is left of the demon to a new Temple sorcerer. Salvaging…something."

"Do you really think it would be that much different than when an elemental is transferred for the first time from an animal to a sorcerer?"

"I am quite sure it would be different. What I don't know is how dangerous it might be to the recipient to take in such a crippled partner."

Pen almost rose to the defense of the vixen by arguing that Hamo wouldn't be talking of sacrifice if the demon had gone into some random *person*. But of course, if it had gone into a person, they'd be able to speak for themselves, human and demon both. Gods, he was too tired to think straight.

"There's a third choice. Leave the vixen with the shamans for a while, let them tame her."

Hamo sat back, startled. "What would be the point of that? They cannot use her demon-spirit for the basis of a Great Beast; the two magics are incompatible. And the longer we wait, the worse the demon's condition may grow. The more of Mags and Svedra to be lost."

"Or what was lost, was lost at the first. Like pouring water into a cup until it overflows, which then remains as full as it can hold. The point is to study a rare situation, at least for a little. The point is, there is time to think about it. The vixen is probably not going anywhere till the cubs are weaned, some weeks at least." Unless the ascendant demon was directly threatened with annihilation. When it surely would try to save itself, and then they'd have a real problem. Well... *another* real problem.

Hamo hesitated. "Did you sense it to be so?"

"I've only observed the vixen briefly. It would take more time than that to perceive ongoing changes." He carefully did not say *deterioration.* Not that he had to.

"Fine if she's stabilized. Not if she hasn't."

Pen shrugged in provisional concession. "You should certainly come out to the Fellowship's menagerie and examine her carefully, before making any irrevocable decisions."

Lips twisting in bemusement, Hamo said, "Penric—are you trying to preserve the life of a *fox*?"

"Magal's demon seems to be doing so," Pen defended this. Weakly, he feared.

Hamo rubbed his eyes. "Feh. I can't... Let us take this up again out there, then. Tomorrow."

"Good idea, sir." At least the man was not dismissing Penric's words outright. Time for a tactful withdrawal, before he fell off this chair onto that lovely, inviting floor.

Hamo stood up to see him out, another hopeful sign. At the door, he lowered his head and murmured, "I would never have compromised my demon, you know. ...I'd have used a knife. Or my bare hands."

Pen couldn't very well feign being appalled when he'd run through similar thought-chains himself. "Not needed now." He mustered a sympathetic smile and signed himself, tapping his lips twice with his thumb in farewell.

IT WAS midnight by the time Pen made his weary way back to the Temple guest house. He was trying to mentally compose a note to slip under the princess-archdivine's door, excusing himself from appearing due to the lateness of the hour, when he discovered a paper pinned to his own. It was in her secretary's fine hand, and charged him to call on her before he retired regardless of the time.

He threaded the halls to her chambers and tapped tentatively, waited, and knocked again. He was just turning away when the door swung open, and the secretary beckoned him inside the sitting room. "Ah, Learned Penric, at last. Wait here."

He stood dumbly in his day dirt, feeling every bruise and muscle-pull. At length, Llewen emerged from an inner door, wrapped in a brocade night robe and with her hair in a gray braid down her back. Not an ensemble he'd seen before.

She looked him over. "My, my, my."

Three *mys* tonight, goodness. He usually rated only two. He wondered what he'd have to do to win four.

"My apologies, Archdivine, for waking you at this hour. It's been a long day."

"At my age, I'm never asleep at this hour." She made a dismissive gesture, charitably fending his apology. Her secretary settled her in a cushioned chair, and her wave directed Pen to another.

Fine blue-and-white silk stripes. He stared at it in dismay, considered his reek, and then settled himself cross-legged on the floor at her feet, instead. Her gray brows rose ironically as she looked down at him.

"So, how was your day in the country this time?"

He was grateful for the practice he'd had recounting it already. He didn't have to think as much. She pressed her fingers to her lips a few times, but did not interrupt him apart from a few shrewd, uncomfortably clarifying questions.

"I thought... I thought I might receive some spiritual guidance from Learned Hamo, as we both share the burden and gift of a demon, but it turned out to be more the other way around," sighed Pen. "Though I don't think he's going to bolt off in the night to try to commit murder on Learned Magal's behalf."

"Was that a risk?"

"Mm...not now."

Her lips twitched. "Then your counsel must have been good enough."

He turned his hands out, smiling ruefully. He really wanted to lie across her silk-slippered feet like a tired dog. "But who will counsel me?"

"Your own Temple superior, of course. That's her job."

"Ah." His head tipped over, and he found himself resting it upon her knee. Her beringed hand petted his hair. Dog indeed.

"Anyone who wishes to question my court sorcerer on his actions today must go through me," she stated. *And good luck to them* stood implied, he thought. Heartening, but...

"So much for the realm, and the law. But what about my god? And my demon. My soul stands more naked in that court. Violence, it appears, grows easier with practice. Or so Halber demonstrates. I've seen it in the ruined mercenary soldiers come back to the cantons, too, sometimes. The pitfall of their trade. I don't want it to become the pitfall of mine. And...and I see how it could. So very, very easily. Hamo was almost ready to slip tonight, and he's had decades more experience than me."

"And thus you seek my counsel?"

"Aye. Archdivine."

Her slow strokes turned into more perfunctory pats, as she sat up and took thought, and then breath. "So. My counsel to you tonight—as your Temple superior, my oh-so-learned divine and demon-burdened boy—is to go downstairs to the guesthouse bathing chamber, wake the attendant, get a bath—wash your *hair*"—her fingers paused to rub together in mild revulsion—"get something to eat, and go to bed." She added after a moment, "Desdemona shall like that, too."

Pen glowered at her slippers. "That's not my Temple superior, that's my *mother*."

"And if she were here, I have no doubt she would tell you the same thing," she said briskly, pushing him upright off her knee despite himself. "Shoo."

"That's *all*?"

"Clean your teeth, I suppose. Though you usually do that without being told. Your soul will keep for one night, I promise you, and your body and mind will be better tomorrow."

He and Des snorted in unison, this time: he at Llewen, Des at him. "Agh." He stretched, and clambered up; he had to balance on his hands and knees before he could rise to his feet. Des had made no interrupting comment throughout this interview. There weren't many people his demon much respected, but Princess-Archdivine Llewen kin Stagthorne was high on that short list. It seemed the feeling was growing mutual.

He commanded over his shoulder as he made for the door, "You go to sleep, too, Your Grace."

She smiled wryly at him. "Oh, I shall be able to now."

PEN HEAVED himself out of bed the next morning thinking the princess-archdivine might have been overly optimistic about how much recovery one night's sleep would provide him. He contemplated the walk all the way down across town and out to the Fellowship, not to mention back up again, and ordered a horse brought around from the Temple mews, instead. It proved another slug, suiting his mood perfectly as he sat atop it in a daze while it ferried him to his destination. By the time he arrived at the palisade and gate of the shamanic menagerie, he had come awake, helped by a cool, moist wind up the valley of the Stork that promised rain.

He handed off his mount to a helpful groom, then found his way to the fox family's stall in the shorter stable block that overlooked the menagerie yard. Lunet was in attendance, he was pleased to discover, sitting on a stool under the broad eaves and looking none the worse for yesterday's wear. She greeted him with good cheer.

Pen asked anxiously, "Does the family seem well, after their forcible relocation?"

"Quite well; take a look."

They both leaned on the lower door and peered into the straw-lined stall. The vixen was laid out looking placid enough, nursing two cubs while three slept curled in a furry mound, and the last tried to stir up trouble by gnawing on what parts of its siblings it could reach. The vixen lifted her head warily at Pen, but laid it back down with a tired maternal sigh. The shamaness, it seemed, worried her not at all.

"The cubs are happy enough, if rambunctious," Lunet told him. "We'll need to let them out for exercise, when we're sure, ah, their mother is settled."

Meaning the vixen, or the demon? The demon was ascendant, there could be no doubt, rider not ridden, if letting the vixen have her way with her family. It wasn't the fox who was dealing so smoothly with their human captors.

Des, thought Pen, *can you discern any change since yesterday in the demon?*

The vixen—no, the demon lifted the vixen's head again as she felt her fellow-demon's uncanny regard, but she tolerated the inspection. That much of her Temple tameness lingered, at least. A hopeful sign?

No new loss since yesterday, Desdemona allowed, *in her density. Calmer, which is good.*

It could be too early to tell. Pen wanted to be able to declare her stabilized, and Des knew why, but he also needed the claim to be true.

Hamo and his lad will be able to judge for themselves, if he gives it some time.

His lad? Oh, Hamo's own demon. *Younger than you, is he?*

Most demons are. Hamo is only his second human rider; he was a mere elemental not long before that. She added a bit grudgingly, *Hamo seems to have been good for him. He has developed quite well. That one could be ready for a physician in one more well-chosen lifetime.*

Always the golden prize, much the way a Great Beast suitable to make a shaman was the goal of the shamans' own carefully reiterated sacrifices. That might make a career for the cubs. The shamans preferred long-lived beasts, to build up spiritual strength and wisdom, so they would certainly prosper better in such care than in the wild, where half the litter would not survive their first year.

Voices carrying through the damp air pulled Pen from his meditations, and he turned to discover Learned Hamo rounding the stable block, accompanied, a bit to his surprise, by Oswyl and his shadow Thala. Oswyl must have gone to exchange reports as promised with Hamo this morning, though Pen rather thought it was curiosity, not duty, that brought him along here.

Oswyl nodded at the shamaness Lunet, who waved back in her usual friendly manner, and punctiliously introduced her to the bailiff of sorcerers.

"I thank you for your hard work yesterday," said Hamo to Lunet, trying to return the civility, but his gaze was drawn inexorably to the stall. "Can I... may I go in?"

Lunet pursed her lips. "Of course, Learned, though we are trying not to disturb the mother fox too much." The hint being that Hamo should withdraw promptly if he did. He nodded understanding, and Lunet drew open the lower door, closing it after him.

The vixen looked up abruptly, then rose and shook off her cubs, who complained and retreated from the human. But her posture did not speak of defense. Hamo fell to his knees before her, then sat cross-legged in the straw. She came to him without fear. Hamo was, Pen realized belatedly, the first person the demon-vixen *could* recognize.

They stared at each other for a long moment. Without speech, but not without understanding, because Hamo placed his hand out flat to the floor and whispered, "I am so sorry for your loss."

Oh. Of course. Of course. Because Learned Magal had lost her demon, but the demon had also lost her Mags. Did demons mourn?

Oh, yes, breathed Des. *It is not something we come into the world knowing, as elementals. But we learn. Oh, how we learn.*

Pen's stomach fluttered in a flash of formless, unanchored grief. Not his own. He had to inhale and exhale carefully.

The vixen placed one black paw atop the man's outstretched hand. Pen needed neither hearing nor Sight to interpret this language: *I am sorry for your loss as well.*

Hamo turned his head to his watchers only long enough to murmur, "She's in there. Something of her is definitely still in there." Then all his attention returned to the animal.

Lunet jerked her chin, and muttered, "They'll be all right. Let's leave them for a little." She, too, felt the sense of intrusion on some painfully private communion, Pen fancied.

In the gray morning light, the four of them went over to the mounting blocks where Pen had first seen the shamans...only yesterday? He, for one, sat with a grunt of relief.

Oswyl looked down at his hands clasped between his knees, and asked, "Do you think he loved her? Hamo and Magal."

Pen made a releasing gesture. "Clearly so, but if you mean a love of the bedchamber, likely not. It would be vanishingly rare for two sorcerers to be so physically intimate. But there are other loves just as profound. Delighting in her as a protégée, hoping for her bright future, all of that. And the future of her demon. Think of two rival artists, perhaps, admiring each other's work. The survivor mourning not just what was, but what could have been."

"Hm."

Thala listened with a thoughtful frown, but for once jotted no notes.

"How of yourselves?" asked Pen. "Did all go well last night, delivering Halber to his fate?" Now doubly earned, and Pen was not above hoping it would prove doubly ill.

Oswyl nodded. "He's in a cell, and in the hands of the justiciars. I doubt he'll be escaping on a fast horse this time around."

"Reports to your superiors go smoothly?" asked Pen, thinking of his own fraught night.

Oswyl actually grinned. Slyly, but still. Pen's brows rose in question.

"I arrived to find them anxious to tell me that my case was to be taken from me and given to a much more senior inquirer, on account of the kin Pikepool connections cropping up. I had to tell them they were too late off the mark."

"Alas," murmured Thala, in the most unrepentant lilt imaginable. She shared the smirk with her senior.

Pen had enough experience with bureaucratic hierarchies by now to have no trouble reading that one, either. "Congratulations."

"Thank you," said Oswyl. "Thank you several times over. Not least that I don't have poor Baron Wegae's corpse on my plate today. That would not have proved nearly so palatable a dish to present." Oswyl's grin turned to grimace with the vision. "He wants to see you again, by the by."

Pen nodded. "I'm sure I can make a chance, before I have to leave Easthome."

Thala asked the air generally, "So, are shamans like sorcerers? Not able to live or work together much?"

"Not at all," said Lunet. "We work together all the time. I have a group singing-practice this afternoon, in fact."

Thala didn't look entirely elated at this news, but asked, "Like a Temple choir?"

Lunet's smile was suddenly all fox. "Not exactly, no."

Combining weirding voices? *Oh my*, as the princess-archdivine might say. Or even, *My, my, my.* Pen *really* wanted to see that.

Lunet stared off at some point over Oswyl's shoulder, and remarked, "Although shamans share some of the problems I suspect sorcerers may have. Ordinary people are afraid to get close to us, afraid of the powers in our blood that they do not understand. As if because we possess strange beasts, we are them."

"That sounds…foolish," said Oswyl in a tentative tone. "If you don't understand something, you should just try to learn more, that's all."

Lunet's gray eyes glinted at him from under her ruddy lashes. Pen could not parse her expression, although Des murmured, *Heh. Not* too *hopelessly thick, that boy.*

Thala looked curiously at Pen, and said, "Then it would seem sorcerers have a doubly lonely time of it. If ordinary people fear them, and other sorcerers cannot be too near them."

That girl saw too much, and said too little, but when she did…ouch. "We always have our demons," Pen offered. He thought Des would have patted his head in approval if she could.

"Ah, you're all here!" came a voice, and Pen turned in some relief to wave at Inglis.

He strolled near and looked them over, almost smiling. "All well this morning with our new foxes?" he asked Lunet.

"Aye. Penric's Learned Hamo came to see them. He's in there now." She gestured toward the stall. "Private conclave."

Inglis paused, extending what shamanic perception Pen did not know, but he nodded. "Right." He looked at Pen. "Will it be all right?"

A comprehensive question, that. "I'll know in a little."

Inglis tapped his fingers on his trouser seam, nodded again at the Grayjays. No, at Thala. "Would you like to look around the menagerie while we wait? I could show you our wolves."

"I'd be quite interested in that," said Thala, rising at once to her feet and almost-smiling back at him.

Lunet's eyes narrowed in merriment, watching this play. She leaned over and said to Oswyl, "And I could show you our other foxes."

"Oh! Ah, you have more?"

"And the lynxes. They're really fine."

Oswyl mustered an actual smile at her, and rose as well, suddenly all amiable cooperation. On Oswyl, it looked very odd.

Rather than departing as a group, the two shamans started to draw the two Grayjays off in opposite directions, though Lunet paused to politely ask over her shoulder, in a most unpressing tone, "And you, Learned Penric?"

He waved her off. "Inglis showed me around the other day. I'll wait here for Hamo."

"Oh, all right."

How very tactful of you, Pen.

As they rounded the corner, Pen could hear Oswyl asking, in an almost-convincing simulation of his habitual inquirer's style, "And how long have you been a member of the Royal Fellowship, Shaman Lunet? How did you become interested in the calling...?"

Hah, murmured Des. *Shamans really do work together.*

Pen watched them out of sight, then sighed, "Don't mind me. I'll just sit here and talk to myself."

Now, now, boy.

Pen's lips twitched.

His smile faded as he studied the silent stall door. This must be what it was like waiting for a judge to return from his chambers and deliver a verdict. He considered extending his Sight, but thought it might be felt as intrusive; it would certainly be felt. Going over and leaning on the stall door would scarcely be better, putting three chaos demons in such close proximity.

At length, his careful patience was rewarded when Hamo emerged, brushing a few straws off his trousers and closing the lower door behind him. He looked around a trifle blindly, then walked over and sat on the mounting block farthest from Pen.

"So?" said Pen quietly. "What do you think?"

"Stable," said Hamo slowly, "for an ascendant demon. Magal's and Svedra's influences lingering, I think. Safe enough for the moment. But I must be careful not to thoughtlessly take this fox for the same thing as a new elemental, ignorant of the uses of its powers. The same marred imprints that make it tamer make it more dangerous. It will require much more shrewd and mindful care."

Pen rubbed his booted toe across the cobblestones. "I was thinking about how the Order sometimes pairs a trained aspirant with an aged sorcerer, to acquaint the demon with its proposed new home in advance." A gruesome deathwatch Pen had been spared by Ruchia's sudden roadside accident, or at any rate, the experience had been compressed to minutes and not weeks or months. "What if, once the vixen has weaned her cubs, she might be given into the care of such an aspirant? It might make for a more gentle transition. And a kinder surveillance."

Hamo tilted his head. "She would make an extraordinary pet," he allowed.

Pen could not only picture it, he envied it. The vixen and her young sorceress-to-be, going about together. If he didn't have a demon already...

You just think it would be madly stylish to have a clever pet fox, Des mocked him. He didn't deny it.

"It would take some careful matchmaking," said Hamo.

This man, Pen was reminded, *made* sorcerers for the Temple. "I expect you're up to that."

"Maybe," said Hamo, his eyes narrowing as he considered Pen knew-not-what pertinent factors. "Maybe. I so want to salvage...I must take some thought who might...hm. Hm."

Pen liked the tone of those *hms*. Very hopeful. By the time the cubs were weaned, Hamo would have had some weeks to scour, really, the whole Weald for suitable candidates, among all the aspirant-divines scattered across the Hallow King's realm. The task, he had no doubt, would be done well, and shrewdly. Somewhere out there was a very lucky aspirant indeed.

Are you regretting the haste and disorder of our own pairing? Des's query was soft, the faintest tint of hurt coloring her doubt. Not that it could be undone now. Save by a few arrows to his back or some like mischance.

Pen returned ruefully, *Oh, I have for a while suspected we had a better Matchmaker than Hamo, conscientious though he is.*

...That thought would be more flattering if it were more comforting.

Aye, Pen sighed.

THE EASTHOME royal magistrates hanged Halber kin Pikepool a week after the Grayjays had returned him to their custody.

Penric did not attend. Hamo did, he heard.

THREE DAYS before they were to depart for Martensbridge, Penric made a formal request to call upon the princess-archdivine.

She received him in her private chambers, waving out the servants attempting to pack all that she had brought, topped by all that she had acquired in the royal capital, for the four-hundred-mile journey home. The Easthome hills were fine in their way, but they were not the austere white peaks fencing his horizon that Pen was used to. Though the mountains, he was sure, would wait for him, with the endless patience of stone. All the impatience of flesh and nerve drove him now.

He flashed his finest smile as he seated himself on blue-and-white silk, safe now against the trousers of his Order's well-laundered whites. "I have a proposal for you, Your Grace. To enhance my abilities as your court sorcerer."

"Shouldn't there be more pleasantries before you leap in?"

"Oh. Er, do you want some?"

"Not particularly." A quirk of her gray eyebrows indicated interest without commitment. "Do go on."

"I've been speaking with my friend Shaman Inglis. And with his superior, Master Firthwyth, over at the Royal Fellowship. He is supervisor of the training of the young shamans. The Fellowship being part school, part farm, part a community of historical scholarship, and part, these days, hospice for injured or sick creatures."

"It sounds a lively place," she conceded.

He nodded vigorously. "Anyway, Master Firthwyth agrees that it would be of great interest for me to study awhile with the royal shamans. Learn what I can of their magics."

"And what do my nephew's shamans gain from this?"

"Well, they get to study me back, I expect."

"How long do you imagine this study would take?"

"Hard to say. I mean, a shaman can spend a lifetime exploring his calling, but I already have a calling of my own, that, er, calls to me as well. But the Fellowship maintains a fine and growing library. I was allowed to see it, when I was over there visiting the other day." Inglis had sternly forbade him to drool on the priceless volumes.

"And how long would it take you to read every book in it? A month?"

"Oh, longer than that!" He hesitated. "…A year?"

"A cap of sorts, I suppose." A quizzical tilt of her elaborately braided head. "And what would my reimbursement be, for the loss of your services during all that time?"

"When I came back, I could do more kinds of things?"

"What things?"

"If I already knew—if anyone knew—I wouldn't have to go study to find out, now would I?"

"That's…actually a less specious argument than it sounds at first blush."

They exchanged nods, like two swordsmen saluting.

She drummed her fingers on her silk-swathed knee. "When we returned home, I was going to tell you…Master Riedel of the Mother's Order in Martensbridge was very impressed by your new edition of Learned Ruchia's work on sorcery as applied to the arts of medicine. He wanted to extend you an invitation to study at the hospice. Part-time, as your other duties permitted."

"*Oh.*" Pen sat up. He hadn't realized his gift of the fresh-printed volumes to the hospice's library, and his few meals at the princess-archdivine's table with Master Riedel, had borne such excellent fruit. "Oh, yes, I'd like to do that! Too."

"Not instead?"

"Too," he said, with more certainty. "Though I grant I can't do both at once. Not even with sorcery."

"Then you have a puzzle." She sat back in some fascination, as if to watch him solve it. Or, possibly, as if to watch a man trying to eat a meal twice the size of his head, Pen wasn't sure.

"Two of Des's prior riders," he said slowly, "had trained and practiced as physicians."

"Master Riedel is aware. He thinks it would make you a very quick study."

Pen nodded. "In my prior experiences with, with drawing on Des's vast knowledge, it doesn't exactly just appear on its own in my mind. I have to induce it, more or less. Like, I don't know, digging a ditch from an irrigation channel to its water source. Then it flows on its own. Well, sometimes it's more like raising it bucket by bucket, but in any case. It was so with the languages. What Master Riedel might teach me would allow me to know all Des knows, eventually."

Pen wasn't going to ask Des's opinion on this one. She'd had her own reasons for jumping to not-yet-Learned Ruchia last time, rather than the physician-aspirant that the Temple had planned for her. Besides, having transcribed every word of Ruchia's medical text for printing, not to mention translating it into two and a half languages so far, he'd gained more than a trickle of understanding already.

"The point is," he slowly felt his way forward, "if I study the shamanic magic first, I will have a chance of bringing something new back to more formal medical studies. More than just a review of things already known."

Llewen pursed her lips. "That is an honestly compelling view." She hesitated. "And how would you plan to support yourself, during this scholarly holiday?"

"I, er, was hoping you could grant me a stipend?"

"So I am to *pay* to be deprived of your services for some undefined amount of time?"

"...Yes?" Pen tried for a sop. "Although I am fairly sure Wegae and Yvaina kin Pikepool would feed me, from time to time. I've already enjoyed some very interesting dinners over there."

"Set a savory table, do they?"

"I don't remember the food. But Yvaina has had this terrific notion, if I can get Learned Hamo interested. She proposes to invest in a press, using the sort of printing plates I produce with sorcery. Except I had this idea, really from rusting out Treuch's knife before he gutted me, well, anyway, explaining it over dinner, it occurred to me that a sorcerer could create steel plates as well as wooden ones. Which could last for thousands of copies, not just dozens or hundreds. So students wouldn't ever have to stab each other over sharing expensive texts again. And then she asked if I couldn't do woodcuts or engravings the same way, and I said no, never thought about it because I couldn't draw, but then she said, maybe some sorcerer who could. And I said, Oh. Of course. I think I can get Hamo to let me teach the technique to some of his people. And then—"

Llewen held up a hand to stem this tide. "Remind me to have my secretary explain the concept of a percentage recompense to you. Soon. Possibly tonight."

"Er, yes, Archdivine." Pen subsided.

"Certainly before you are turned loose in Easthome to cut whatever swathe seems inevitable."

Pen's heart rose in hope. In quite another tone, he said, "*Yes*, Archdivine."

"Hah." She rubbed her fine chin, regarding him thoughtfully. "There is a line from a poem that rises to my mind. I no longer remember from where, but that's the hazard of my years—oh. Do you suppose Baroness kin Pikepool's press would ever share out poetry?"

Pen sat nonplussed, then afire. "I was thinking of texts, but certainly, why not? Or maybe books of tales... Really, anything." He paused, wanting to ask what she would offer for a stipend, but his curiosity was caught. "What was the verse?"

"Just a fragment, really. A call-and-response song. The bard was describing an itinerant scholar. 'Joyfully he learned/joyously taught.' Went about in rags, poor man, which I thought quite unfair."

"Probably had spent all his money on copyists. One must make choices, after all."

She snorted, delicately. But then asked, "And what does Desdemona think of all this?"

Pen started to open his mouth, then said, "Des?" yielding control of his speech to her.

"I'm for the shamans," said Des without hesitation. "It will be something new. Also, Ruchia has some very fond memories of one."

Pen shut his mouth again quickly, before she could go into the more ribald details. And then wondered what (possibly horrifying) conversations Des and Llewen might get into if he wasn't around, listening in.

Surely you must test that, Des quipped. He tightened his teeth.

Llewen tapped his hand. "Just bring him back to me, Desdemona."

"As you wish, Archdivine," agreed the demon.